DEATH OF AN EFFENDI

Cairo, 1909. The murder capital of the world, where deaths are two a piastre. But the death of an effendi? That is something different. Because effendis – the Egyptian elite – are important. Especially if – in a country ruled by foreigners – they happen to be foreign.

When Tvardovsky, an effendi and foreigner, is shot at a gathering of financiers, Gareth Owen – the Mamur Zapt, Chief of Cairo's Secret Police – is called to investigate. But is he the right man for the job? In some countries, if someone goes for a walk, or a boat ride, with the Head of the Secret Police and doesn't come back, it's best not to ask any questions. And there are powerful people who might have preferred Tvardovsky dead.

As the maverick financier said, before going on the fatal shooting party, there were still crocodiles in Egypt. Of all kinds. And perhaps the place to look for them was Crocodilopolis, the ancient City of the Crocodiles, where the financiers were to hold their meeting. It is when the crocodiles start cooperating, said Tvardovsky, that you really have to watch out . . .

DEATH OF
AN EFFENDI

A MAMUR ZAPT MYSTERY

Michael Pearce

HarperCollins*Publishers*

Collins Crime
An imprint of HarperCollins*Publishers*
77–85 Fulham Palace Road, London W6 8JB

First published in Great Britain
in 1999 by Collins Crime

1 3 5 7 9 10 8 6 4 2

Copyright © Michael Pearce 1999

Michael Pearce asserts the moral right to
be identified as the author of this work

A catalogue record for this book
is available from the British Library

ISBN 0 00 232685 X

Set in Meridien and Bodoni
by Palimpsest Book Production Limited,
Polmont, Stirlingshire

Printed and bound in Great Britain by
Caledonian International Book Manufacturing Ltd, Glasgow

DEATH OF
AN EFFENDI

1

'Of course, it's very quiet there,' said Owen.

'Just what we want!'

'And picturesque. Flamingoes, pelicans, that sort of thing.'

'Excellent!'

'No crocodiles there now,' said McPhee.

'Crocodiles!'

Owen sometimes wished that McPhee would keep his mouth shut.

'There used to be,' said McPhee. 'In fact, the lake was famous for them. They were kept almost as pets. The priests used to pamper them, prepare special feasts for them –'

'Crocodiles!' said the man from the Khedive's office uneasily. 'I don't think His Highness will be happy about that!'

'There aren't any now,' said Owen, perspiring. They had been going round and round in the meeting all morning trying to hit on a place and just when they'd got one, that bloody fool of a Deputy Commandant –

'The whole area was sacred to the crocodile god once,' said McPhee happily. 'That's why they named the town after it. Crocodilopolis.'

'It sounds a most unsuitable place to me,' said the official. 'I'm sure His Highness wouldn't want to stay –'

'He couldn't,' Owen almost shouted, 'even if he wanted to! It's all under the sand!'

'Uncomfortable, too? No, really –'

'It was under the sand three thousand years ago!'

'Oh, come, Owen,' McPhee objected mildly. 'Two thousand.'

'Two thousand. In the past, anyway. *There are no crocodiles there now.*'

'How do you know?' objected the man from the Khedive's office. 'I thought all the lake was fed by the Bahr-el-Yussuf flowing westward from the Nile. Couldn't crocodiles swim along it?'

'There aren't any crocodiles in the Nile *either*,' said Owen. 'Not these days. Not since the dam was built at Aswan. There *couldn't be.*'

'Or suppose they'd just stayed there? In the lake, I mean. Stayed there and bred?'

'Someone would have seen them.'

'*Has* anyone seen them?'

'Well, Strabo reports –' began McPhee.

'Strabo? Is he one of your men?'

McPhee looked at him, astonished. 'Strabo died two thousand years ago,' he said.

'Surely you have more up-to-date information?' said the official.

'I have,' said Owen wearily. 'The spot we are proposing is on the shore of Lake Karun. Where there is a luxury hotel. And good shooting and fishing. And no crocodile has been seen in a thousand years.'

'You are sure about the shooting? The Consul was very specific on that point.'

'Yes.'

The official eyed the clock. It was getting close to siesta time.

'I suppose we could settle, then,' he said reluctantly. 'If you are sure about the crocodiles.'

'Quite sure.'

'Very well, then. It's just that we wouldn't want an unfortunate mishap. His Highness was very insistent about that. There is to be no unfortunate incident, he said.'

* * *

2

The party left Cairo early in the morning by train and arrived at Wasta just over an hour later. At Wasta they changed to a branch line which took them to Medinet-el-Fayoum. At Medinet they took the light railway to Abchaway, where an assortment of carriages was waiting for them.

They drove for an hour through a countryside which, although Owen had now lived in Egypt for several years was unfamiliar to him. What he knew was city and sand and river. But here were fertile green fields, burgeoning with grapes, figs, apricots, olives, corn and cotton and bursting with roses. Everywhere the fields were crossed by little canals and in the distance was a long turquoise streak which gradually revealed itself to be a lake.

The hotel was a row of roomy square tents along a stone terrace above the lake. Tied up to the bank were boats of all sorts, some rowing, some sailing, some as old as the Pharaohs, woven out of reeds, mere baskets on the water pushed along by paddles.

The vehicles stopped and the guests were shown to their tents by stooping, scarlet-cummerbunded suffragis. Afterwards, a cold lunch was served beneath the palm trees. Wines – not the perfectly respectable wine of the district but from Burgundy and the Loire – accompanied the food and beside each table was a bucket filled with ice and containing a welcoming bottle of champagne.

For this was no ordinary shooting party. When Nuri Pasha, Zeinab's father, had heard who was to be present, his eyes had widened.

'My dear boy,' he had said, 'you don't think you could wangle me an invitation?'

But that was something that even the Mamur Zapt, Head of the Khedive's Secret Police, could not do. Indeed, what he himself was doing there was open to question.

Tvardovsky was sitting at the table next to Owen. He was sitting alone, looking out over the lake, crumbling his bread roll nervously. Sweat was running down his face; where his hand had rested on the tablecloth there was a damp patch. He dabbed at his forehead with his napkin, then wiped round above his collar.

Suddenly, he threw down the napkin, got to his feet and walked down to the water. Owen gave it a moment and then went down to join him.

'Why do they have to kill?' demanded Tvardovsky.

'Kill?'

Tvardovsky gestured towards the ducks nosing peacefully in and out among the reeds.

'Why don't they just leave them alone?'

Owen looked back up at the tables, at the pale, fat men in their new tropical suits and with their new sun helmets parked cautiously on the ground beside them, and laughed.

'Looking at the marksmen,' he said. 'I think there's a fair chance they'll miss.'

Tvardovsky laughed too, a short, fierce laugh, more like a bark than a laugh.

'They don't usually,' he said.

Some men had joined the group up on the terrace: His Highness himself and some of the princes, the Minister of Finance, the Governor of the Bank of Egypt, the Chairman of the British Chamber of Commerce and the Financial Adviser. His Highness seated himself in a plush red armchair and a man Owen didn't know but guessed to be the new Russian Consul began to go round the tables bringing up their occupants for presentation to him. Afterwards, they were drawn aside into conversation with the other members of his party. There was no problem about language; all the Russians spoke French, as did, as a matter of course, all the Egyptian upper classes and all the senior officials.

Owen had thought that Tvardovsky might be out of it but when he saw the new arrivals he hurried back up to the terrace and inserted himself beside the Financial Adviser, who was, certainly, in this assembly, the man to talk to.

Owen returned to his table and went on with his lunch.

Gradually the tables emptied and there was a general cluster in the middle around His Highness's party.

After a while, Owen became aware that he was not the only one remaining on the periphery. At the table next to his was a woman in her early thirties, tall, slim, blonde and dressed in jodhpurs, an embroidered blouse and, incongruously, a dark veil.

'I've been wondering about you,' she said. 'You're not one of us and yet you don't seem to be one of them. Which side are you on?'

'I'm not on anyone's side,' said Owen, 'who's anything to do with finance. They won't have me. Wisely.'

'Dear, dear!' said the woman. 'I have a feeling you won't get far in life.'

She belonged, presumably, to one of the financiers.

'So what are you doing here?' she asked.

'Oh, I'm just here in a general capacity,' said Owen, 'as one of the Khedive's servants.'

The woman looked at him closely, then laughed.

'I understand,' she said. 'We have them too. People who serve the Tsar. In a general capacity.'

That evening there was a reception for the shooting party. Waiters moved among them carrying silver trays on which were thin-stemmed glasses of sherry, cut-glass tumblers of whisky and some other glasses containing a colourless liquid: vodka, Owen supposed, in deference to the visitors' tastes.

One of the princes, Fuad, came across to him.

'Not drinking?'

'No.'

'I suppose not.' He looked across the terrace. 'How's Tvardovsky?'

'All right. So far.'

The prince considered.

'I think he's an egg,' he said.

'I beg your pardon?'

'An expensive Fabergé egg; but cracked.'

Owen found it hard to get to sleep that night. Partly it was the mosquito netting rigged up around the bed, which made it very hot. A sensible precaution, no doubt, in view of the proximity to water, but one that Owen, in Cairo, was accustomed to doing without. Partly, though, it was the noise the hyenas were making. He could hear them laughing all along the shore.

He slipped out of his bed and went to the door of the tent. Outside, the moonlight made it as bright as day. In Tvardovsky's tent, however, next to his, there was a lamp still on. He stepped across and put his ear to the flap. Tvardovsky seemed to be working. He heard the rustle of papers and from time to time a low exclamation, as if the Russian was surprised at what he found.

Owen went back to his tent. Out behind the reeds the moon was silvering the water. A puff of wind ruffled the leaves of the palm trees along the terrace and a moment later broke up the silver into myriads of glittering fragments. Owen thought he heard the plop of a fish.

Over by the kitchen there was a sudden shout and then, clear in the moonlight, Owen saw a hyena loping away, carrying something in its mouth. Whoever had shouted did not bother to chase it and soon, out in the shadows, Owen heard the crack as the creature's powerful jaws got to work.

And now there was a different noise. From one of the tents further along the row he could hear a woman's soft moans. Well, that was what she was there for, presumably.

The moans quickened, became urgent and then sighed away, and then for a while all was quiet. Owen wondered whether to go back to bed but knew that if he went back too soon he would stay awake. He thought about going down to the lake. But there was always Tvardovsky.

He heard someone moving among the tents and then, to his surprise, for he had assumed she was otherwise engaged, he saw the blonde woman. She was wearing a long black kimono. Her feet were bare. He stepped back from the doorway. There was a swish of silk as she went past. Outside Tvardovsky's tent she hesitated and then went in.

There were no moans this time, just what appeared to be a short, intense argument in a language Owen did not understand. Then the woman came out again, so quickly that he had no time to step back. She saw him standing there and smiled.

The next morning, after breakfast, the waiters arranged some armchairs beneath the palms and the financiers continued their discussion. Owen stayed on the terrace at his breakfast table. After a while, one of the waiters, a young, pleasant-looking man, came up to him.

'You no talking?' he said in English.

'No.'

'Why no talking?'

'They're talking about money.'

The waiter smiled.

'You not got?'

'That's right,' said Owen. 'Not got.'

The waiter squatted down on his haunches, ready to drift into conversation in the easy way of the Egyptians. The pressure was off the waiters now and he could afford to relax.

'Me, too,' he said. 'Not got.'

'Got wife yet?'

The waiter looked glum.

'Money first,' he said. 'Then wife.'

'Same here.'

That was not quite true. There were other reasons preventing, or perhaps delaying, his and Zeinab's marriage: the attitude the British Administration would probably take to one of its servants marrying an Egyptian, for a start. But then, Zeinab herself was uncertain. Did she want to marry an Englishman?

'Welshman,' pleaded Owen.

As Zeinab was not quite sure about the difference between

7

the two, that made her even more uncertain. She knew that Wales was, or had been, like Egypt, an independent country and that, like Egypt, it had been conquered by the English. But where did that leave Owen? Was he, like so many young Egyptians, a secret Nationalist? But if so, how did he come to be Mamur Zapt? And what would happen when they found out? If Zeinab was doubtful about marrying one of the conquering English, she – ever the realist – was even more doubtful about marrying one of the losing Welsh, particularly, if as seemed to be the case, there was more than an outside chance that the English might garotte him.

The real obstacle, however, Owen suspected, was that having invested so much willpower in creating a life for herself as an independent woman, which took some doing in Egypt, she hadn't got quite enough left to take the last step, making an independent marriage.

But would her father, Nuri, in fact object? He and Owen had always got along well. But getting on well was one thing, marrying a daughter quite another. Pashas like Nuri tended to view marriage as a means of political and financial alliance. It might suit him for the moment to have his daughter close to the Head of the Khedive's Secret Police but that advantage would be only as temporary as a civil servant's career. As for financial advantage, Nuri knew only too exactly how little Owen earned. So, yes, it was true what he had said to the waiter: they were in the same boat.

The waiter jerked his thumb in the direction of the financiers.

'They lot of money,' he said. 'Why they want more?'

'That's the way of rich men,' said Owen.

'True,' acknowledged the waiter, still brooding, however. 'But why they here?'

'Egypt not got,' said Owen.

That was even more true. In fact, it was so true that Egypt's international creditors had felt obliged to set up a commission, the Caisse, to make sure that they were repaid. The British had been installed, or installed themselves, as managers on behalf of the commission, and now it was a good question who really ran the country; the Khedive, Egypt's nominal ruler, the British Consul-General, whose hand was on all the strings, or the Caisse.

The waiter was silent.

'Egypt rich country,' he said after a while, the sweep of his hand taking in the fields with their cotton and sugar cane and fruit. 'Why not got?'

'Ah, well,' said Owen. 'You'll have to ask the Khedive.'

The waiter went into the hotel and returned with a newspaper, which he gave to Owen. It was a copy of *Al-Liwa*, the leading Arabic Nationalist paper. Ordinarily, he would have read it the previous night – one of the Mamur Zapt's duties was to read all the newspapers – before publication – but because he had been away he had not been able to.

He looked at the newspaper and felt vexed. They had slipped up in his absence. There on the front page was a reference to the financiers' visit. What were they here for, demanded *Al-Liwa*? Was it to suck yet more blood out of Egypt's already dried-up veins? Well, if blood was what they wanted, blood was what they would –

Owen gave the newspaper back to the waiter. He was used to the sanguinary rhetoric of the Nationalist newspapers and it did not bother him. However, they had been trying to keep the visit secret. The negotiations were important and neither the British Administration nor the Khedive wanted them disturbed by any unfortunate incident.

'Not got,' said the waiter, jerking his thumb again, 'because all money go out of country to people like them!'

If even ordinary waiters were saying such things, thought Owen, was it any wonder that other people were?

Tvardovsky kept, or was kept, apart from the other Russians. At lunch he came and sat with Owen.

'How's it going?'

'They have no vision,' said Tvardovsky. 'They see only roubles.'

'What do you see?'

'I see fields of grain,' said Tvardovsky. 'This was once Rome's granary. It could be again.'

'Depending on what?'

'Water,' said Tvardovsky, 'and pumps.'

'And money?'

'Well, naturally.'

'People, too,' said Owen.

'Yes,' granted Tvardovsky, 'people are important.' He looked at Owen. 'You know the country,' he said. 'How would the people feel?'

'I think they would need to feel part of it,' said Owen.

'And at the moment they don't,' said Tvardovsky. 'That is because they are serfs.'

'Well, not really –'

'The next best thing to. We were serfs, too, in Russia,' said Tvardovsky. 'I was one. Or, rather, the son of one. So I know.'

'I don't think it's quite the same in Egypt.'

'They need to feel part of it. Will the British make them feel part of it?'

'We have done a bit,' said Owen.

'No,' said Tvardovsky. 'The answer is no. But Russians could.'

Owen looked at the financiers on the adjoining tables.

'You said they had no vision.'

'Not these.' Tvardovsky dismissed them with a contemptuous wave of his hand. 'Others. Have you heard of a Russian named Kropotkin?'

'No,' said Owen.

'He is a prince. But an unusually intelligent one. He says that cooperation, not competition, is the natural way of things. You British will not make the ordinary Egyptian feel part of things because you believe in competition. But that is not what the ordinary man wants. It is not natural to him. What is natural is cooperation. And that is what is needed here.'

'And Mr Kropotkin will bring it?'

'Alas,' said Tvardovsky. 'It may take a bit of time.'

After lunch the financiers, unused to the heat, returned to their tents for a siesta. Owen took a chair, however, and sat outside beneath an orange tree, where the foliage was thick enough to give dense shade. He could have gone back to his tent, next to Tvardovsky's, but from here he could see better.

At about four the financiers began to emerge from their tents and make their way to the armchair area, where they were served afternoon tea. They drank their tea, as the Egyptians did, without milk.

From time to time someone came and led one of them off. Individual interviews had been arranged with the Governor of the Bank of Egypt and the Financial Adviser. 'In the end,' said Tvardovsky, 'a financier has to work alone. We do not trust each other.'

Tvardovsky went for an interview, too. Owen accompanied him to the tent but did not go in.

Dinner was early in view of the shoot the next day. Tvardovsky sat at Owen's table again. He drank heavily.

'Steady on,' said Owen. 'We're making an early start tomorrow, remember.'

'Ah yes,' said Tvardovsky. 'The killing.'

It was still dark but in the tents the lamps were on. Suffragis hurried about carrying bowls of hot water for shaving and coffee for those who needed it. Up on the terrace a light breakfast had been prepared but the main breakfast would be later, after the shoot. People were already walking down to the water.

Owen emerged from his tent carrying a gun. Tvardovsky, coming out at the same time, regarded it distrustfully.

'What's that for?' he said.

'Protective camouflage,' said Owen. He did not expect to use it. Duck-shooting was not what he was about.

Tvardovsky himself was gunless. Nevertheless, he walked down to the boats with the others.

They were flat-bottomed boats, like punts, suitable for the shallow water at the edge of the lake and for lying among the reeds. The boatman held the boats for the shooters to clamber in, two to a boat, with a boatman there to paddle and retrieve.

At the last moment there was a hitch. There were not enough boats to accommodate everyone.

'I'll sit this one out,' said Tvardovsky.

'So will I,' said Owen.

'No, no,' said the maître d'hôtel. 'No problem.'

He produced two more boats. They were of the basket sort, made of reeds. Empty, they seemed to lie on top of the water. Carrying someone, they sank down and water seeped in through the sides so that there was a little pool of water inside the boat, in which the person was sitting. After that, though, they sank down no more and the level of water remained the same, matching that outside.

'Actually,' said the maître d'hôtel, 'you'll find them more suited for shooting. The boatmen will be able to take you right in among the reeds and you'll get a better shot.'

Tvardovsky shrugged and climbed in. That was the snag. The boat could only take him, not Owen. Owen was being marshalled towards a similar boat lying alongside. Tvardovsky looked up at Owen.

'I won't be far,' said Owen.

Tvardovsky shrugged again.

'Where gun?' said the boatman.

'No gun,' said Tvardovsky.

'No gun?' The boatman turned to the maître d'hôtel, bewildered.

'No gun,' said the maître d'hôtel. 'Just watch.'

The boatman exchanged glances with the man holding Owen's boat. The shrugs were ever so slight.

Owen got into his basket. At once the water seemed to rush in.

'All right,' said the boatman, grinning. 'Not sink.'

For a moment Owen was not so sure about that; nor about the general stability of the craft. It rocked crazily and he grabbed at the plaited gunwales on either side. Then the boat settled. He found himself sitting in water. After the first shock it was not disagreeable: pleasantly warm, almost languorous – sensuous, even. He settled the gun between his knees.

Then he remembered and cursed. He felt down into his pocket. Never mind that gun, it was the other one that mattered. He pulled it out, dried it against his tunic and then stuck it into his breast pocket.

His boatman gaped.

'This one,' he said, tapping the gun between Owen's knees. He pointed to the small arm. 'No need,' he said, shaking his head.

'I hope you're right,' said Owen. It hadn't felt very wet. He hoped the chamber had not been affected.

The boatman pushed the boat out and then got in. He began to paddle.

In the other boats the boatmen stood up and poled their craft along. This close to the shore the water was very shallow and the trick was not to get out but to get in, among the reeds. This was where the basket boats had the advantage. The other boats had to hold themselves out on the edge of the reeds. The basket boats could go right in.

The boatman pushed the reeds aside with his paddle and edged through. Tvardovsky's boat was just ahead of them.

'You stay close to that,' Owen directed.

The boatman nodded.

The reeds had closed all around them so that it was as if they were in a little enclave of their own. All they could see was the sky, which was, of course, all that they needed to see.

They settled down to wait. While they had been paddling out there the darkness had cleared and the sun was just coming up over the top of the reeds, a great ball of red.

The reeds were very still. But then, as the sun came up

13

and the warmth began to touch the water, there were little rustles of movement. The lake was waking up.

The boatman reached forward and touched the gun.

Owen shook his head.

The boatman mimicked putting it to his shoulder and firing.

'He doesn't like shooting,' said Owen in Arabic, jerking his head in Tvardovsky's direction. 'He just wants to watch.'

The boatman shrugged, accepting.

Tvardovsky sat sombrely in his boat, a little apart from Owen. Owen tried to catch his eye but Tvardovsky was staring into the reeds.

Suddenly there was a loud report and then from all along the shore, birds flew up into the sky. For a moment all was confusion as the birds scattered and squawked but then there were more reports and suddenly, from over to their right, the ducks came flying. They came with almost unbelievable speed, heading right across their front and out towards the centre of the lake.

At once, raggedly, almost in panic, the shooting started. From somewhere very near them, just beyond the reeds, a veritable barrage opened up.

Tvardovsky put his hands over his ears. The noise was deafening.

The fusillade seemed to have no effect on the ducks. They just flew on and on, an endless number of them.

But then suddenly they were gone. The shooting died away. The lake returned to its quietness. It was as if nothing had happened; only now, here and there among the reeds, Owen saw bunches of feathers and in the water the occasional floating spot of red.

The boatman gave an exclamation and then paddled the boat swiftly to one side. He poked the reeds apart with his paddle, reached out and lifted a bird, hanging limply, into the boat. He paused for a second, eyes searching the reeds and then drove the boat on again, just a few yards. Another bird was handed into the boat.

And then, surprisingly, two last birds came in towards them.

'Effendi, Effendi!'

The boatman thrust the gun into Owen's hands.

Almost without thinking, Owen put the gun to his shoulder and fired.

The birds swooped on and he thought for a moment that he had missed. Then first one and then the other seemed to check in mid flight and fall like stones.

The boatman whooped with delight and hurried the boat to where they had fallen and Owen was pleased, too, exhilarated. He had not meant to take part but then it had all happened so quickly, and he had not been able to resist.

The boatman retrieved the birds and showed them to Owen, smiling. Then he stowed them away with the other birds.

'Hotel?' he said, picking up the paddle.

'Tvardovsky,' said Owen, looking around him. 'Where's Tvardovsky?'

Everywhere were reeds. There was no sight of Tvardovsky.

'The other boat,' said Owen. 'I need to find the other boat!'

The boatman shrugged but then reluctantly began to paddle back in roughly the direction they had come. Only, among the reeds, the direction was no longer clear. In this part of the lake they reached to head-high and grew so thickly that you could not see more than a yard or two in any direction.

'Tvardovsky!' Owen called. 'Where are you?'

But there was no reply.

'Ahmed!' called the boatman. 'Ahmed!'

From somewhere further off they could hear the sounds of the other boats returning, the delighted chatter of the sportsmen.

And then, floating out from behind the reeds, dyeing the water, came a little trail of red; not from a bird this time.

2

Reactions afterwards were strangely muted. His Highness had, fortunately, departed the previous evening. His office issued a statement of regret on his behalf but otherwise seemed surprisingly unconcerned.

'As long as it's kept out of the newspapers,' they said offhandedly.

The Russians took a similar view.

'These things happen,' the Russian Consul said philosophically, 'especially at shooting parties.'

The party itself dispersed after breakfast – a good, solid breakfast for the hunters, with grapefruit fresh from the tree, fish fresh from the lake, and devilled kidneys which were not fresh at all but seemed somehow appropriate.

The Khedive's party left with them, including the princes, who had quite enjoyed the morning's excitement but now that it was over saw no point in staying. Prince Fuad alone remained behind to wrap things up.

The authorities had, of course, been notified immediately and shortly after breakfast the local Mudir appeared. He came with an air of resignation, clearly expecting the worst. The little experience that he had had of dealing with the great had taught him that was what you usually got.

'There's been an accident,' said Prince Fuad peremptorily.

The Mudir spread his hands in deprecation.

So he had heard. Regrettable, he said, keeping his eyes fixed firmly on the ground in front of Prince Fuad's feet. Yes, regrettable. Very. And of an effendi, too? Even more regrettable. But every cloud had a silver lining. At least, so he gathered, it was of a foreign effendi.

'What difference does that make?' demanded Prince Fuad.

Well, said the Mudir, gaining in confidence, or, possibly, garrulous through nervousness, it wasn't like losing one of your own family. It wasn't even like losing an ordinary Egyptian –

His voice died away as his lowered eyes suddenly caught sight of the Russian Consul standing beside Prince Fuad.

On the other hand, he babbled, desperately switching tack, the death of an effendi was always terrible. Even a foreign effendi. No, no – with sighing heart – that was not what he had meant –

'What did you mean?' asked Prince Fuad unkindly.

Well, floundered the Mudir, it wasn't like the death of a mere fellah. Or – his eye scanned desperately – one of the waiters, say. That would have been of no account at all.

There Prince Fuad agreed entirely.

'This was of an effendi, though,' he pointed out.

Exactly! And that was why he, a humble Mudir, was glad to come and offer his services –

'An accident,' said Prince Fuad. 'Got that? Right. Well, off you go –'

Owen was moved to protest.

Oughtn't the Mudir at least speak to the boatman? After all, he had been in the boat when –

'Why not?' said the prince, looking at his watch. 'And you go along with him to see he doesn't get it wrong.'

The boatman, Ahmed, was still in a state of shock. He had been sitting opposite Tvardovsky, holding the boat still as the birds flew over. He had been noting the birds and seeing where they fell when suddenly he had become aware that Tvardovsky had slumped sideways and was hanging over the side of the boat and there was blood trickling down into the water, and blood seeping into the water in the bottom of the boat and blood trickling on to the boatman's foot and –

And by this time it was pretty clear that they were not going to get much more out of *him*.

Owen made a last try.

Had he been conscious of the shot?

There had been so many shots. It had been just when the birds were flying over, at the height of the fusillade, in fact. He had not been conscious of any one particular shot, still less of the shot that had –

He began to shake uncontrollably.

'Well, there you are,' said Prince Fuad, who had joined them. 'It was just when everyone was shooting and one of the shots went astray. That's the trouble with amateurs. The shots could go anywhere. I said as much to His Highness. It's not like a shoot in Scotland, I said – I had some very good shooting there last year with Lord Kilcrankie – when everyone knows what they're doing. Anything could happen! Well, I think he took my point, and that's why he stayed away. Just as well, we wouldn't have wanted him getting mixed up in this kind of thing, would we? Would we?' he asked the Mudir suddenly.

The Mudir, too, began to shake uncontrollably.

'No,' he managed to get out at last.

'Of course, we had to have the shoot, though,' said the prince, as they were walking away. 'The Russians were absolutely insistent on it.'

They returned to the terrace.

'He's quite satisfied,' Prince Fuad informed the Russian Consul. 'Definitely an accident.'

'Oh, good,' said the Consul.

'What else could it be?' asked the Financial Adviser.

Owen made one last effort.

'What about the guns? Oughtn't we to call them in? Then the bullet could be checked against the guns to find out which –'

'Oh, I don't think that's necessary!' interrupted Prince Fuad.

'Indeed not!' cried the Russian Consul. 'Think of the embarrassment it could cause!'

'Well, yes, but –'

'It was obviously an accident. What's the point of apportioning blame?'

The Mudir was only too anxious not to apportion blame. He took Tvardovsky's name and a few particulars from the Russian Consul and then made tracks as fast as he possibly could.

The incident, though unfortunate, might well have been forgotten had it not been for an unusual feature of the legal system. Under the Egyptian legal code, which was modelled on the French one, investigation of a potential crime was the responsibility not of the police but of the Department of Prosecutions of the Ministry of Justice, the Parquet, as it was known. The police would notify the Parquet of the circumstances and the Parquet would then decide whether they merited formal investigation, in which event a Parquet officer would be assigned to the case.

In the provinces the system was slightly different. The police came under the local governor, the Mudir, as he was called, and it was he who had the formal responsibility of notifying the Parquet when a crime was suspected.

The Mudir had, then, notified the Parquet of Tvardovsky's death. Strictly speaking – or, rather, loosely speaking, which was the way more normal in the provinces – no notification was required as the death was the result of an accident. However, as the Mudir himself had remarked, the death of an effendi was different and it had loomed sufficiently large in his mind for him to include it in a report. The Parquet officer who had read the report had written back requesting further details. When these did not satisfy him, he announced that he was opening a formal investigation.

'Of course,' said the British Consul-General's aide-de-camp, as he and Owen were walking into the hastily summoned meeting together, 'it would have to be Mahmoud!'

19

In a country which tended to take a relaxed view of the conduct of business, Mahmoud El Zaki was an exception; although if you had said so he would have taken umbrage. He resented slights on his country. In private, however, he had to admit there was some truth in the charge; and, therefore, to make up for any deficiency he always worked with twice the zeal of anyone else.

'Well, of course,' said Prince Fuad huffily, 'the Ministry of Justice can do just what it likes.'

That, unfortunately, was just what it couldn't do: firstly, because the Minister was an appointee of the Khedive, who would speedily appoint someone else if the Minister showed too many signs of independence; secondly, because at the top of every Ministry, sitting next to the Minister, Egyptian, was an Adviser, British, whose advice it was unwise not to follow.

The Minister muttered something about judicial process once started being hard to stop.

'Nonsense!' said Prince Fuad. 'The question is: who is boss? That's all! Are we the process's masters or its servants?'

'Well,' said the Minister unhappily.

'Well,' said the Adviser.

'Mamur Zapt?'

Owen hesitated. It was sometimes difficult serving two masters: the Khedive, to whom in theory he was responsible, and the British, who had put him there.

'Ordinarily,' he said, 'I would side with Prince Fuad. However, I think that in this case we have to remember that the eyes of the world may be upon us. This was the death of someone who was being invited in to invest in Egypt's prosperity, and if we seem to be taking it too lightly, other investors may be deterred.'

'I do think the Mamur Zapt has a point there!' declared the aide-de-camp.

'So do I!' said the Adviser.

'I'm afraid so,' murmured the Minister.

'Well,' said Prince Fuad crossly, seeing that he was out-gunned, 'what are we going to do about it, then? Couldn't you tell your people merely to go through the motions?' he asked the Minister. 'I mean, that's what they usually do, don't they?'

The Minister murmured something about the officer in question being particularly zealous.

'Would you like me to speak to him?' demanded Prince Fuad.

'No!' said the Minister, who knew Mahmoud and knew that if Prince Fuad spoke to him in his usual way, he was likely to speak back.

'I agree,' said the aide-de-camp quickly. 'The less the Khedive's office is seen to have to do with this, the better!'

'There's something in that,' conceded Prince Fuad. 'However, we are still left with the question of what we're going to do. We can't just leave the Parquet to run wild on a thing like this.'

'Nor should we,' said the aide-de-camp. 'I have a suggestion. This is the death not just of an effendi but of a foreign effendi. Given the circumstances, it is likely that if a case comes to court, it will fall under the Capitulations.' The Capitulations were a system of privileges granted to foreign powers which, among other things, gave their citizens the right to be tried under their own national courts. 'Would it not be wiser if a representative of the Capitulatory Powers was associated with the case from the start?'

'That would certainly please the Russians,' said the Adviser.

'It would have to be someone we could trust,' said Prince Fuad.

'Quite so; and for that reason I was thinking of someone in the service of the Khedive who would also be acceptable to the Powers: the Mamur Zapt.'

'You've landed me in it,' said Owen accusingly, as he walked away from the meeting with the aide-de-camp.

'You were already landed,' said the aide-de-camp, Paul, whom he had hitherto considered his friend.

'You do not usually join me in my investigations,' said Mahmoud. 'Why this one?'

'An important person, I suppose.'

'And yet they seemed prepared to let the whole matter drop.'

'I think they would have let it drop if you hadn't started asking questions.'

'But is not an important person an important person whether I ask questions or not?'

'I think the important thing may be that he was foreign.'

'But that is wrong. The law is the same whether a man is foreign or not.'

'Quite.'

'Or should be.'

'Exactly so.'

They were waiting on the platform of the Gare Centrale. On learning that Owen was going to join him in his inquiries, Mahmoud, scrupulous as ever, had sent him a note saying that he was going down to the Fayoum to see the spot where the incident had occurred and inviting him to accompany him.

'What was it in the report that made you ask questions?' asked Owen.

Mahmoud looked slightly ashamed.

'I was angry,' he admitted. 'It was such a slack piece of work. An accident, yes, but even with an accident there are details that should be included. The death of a visitor to our country, a guest, you could say – one needs to be satisfied. All the more when it is a shooting. An accident, maybe, but even when the shooting is accidental, someone is responsible. The Mudir made no effort to find out who had fired the gun. That is deplorable. He should have called in the guns at least –'

'I did suggest that.'

'You did?'

22

'Yes. They didn't feel it was necessary.'

'Who didn't feel it was necessary?'

'Prince Fuad. The Russian Consul.'

'What is it to do with them?'

'Strictly speaking, nothing, I suppose. However, if you're a humble Mudir –'

'I know, I know.' Mahmoud frowned. 'But it is wrong all the same,' he burst out excitedly – dereliction of duty always excited him. 'A Mudir should have pride, he should have a sense of his responsibilities, he should –'

Mahmond stopped and shook his head.

'I know,' he said. 'He is only a Mudir after all. And in the provinces the older relationships still –'

He stopped again.

'But that is what is wrong! It is what is wrong with the country, too. There is still the old deference to the Khedive, to the Pashas. It gets in the way of doing things properly. And until we start doing things properly, what hope has the country of advancing? All right, he is only a Mudir, but –'

'Even if he had called the guns in,' said Owen placidly, 'all that it probably would have shown us was that it was one of the financiers. And I don't think they were very anxious to show that.'

'But that, too, is wrong. You cannot have the law applying to some people and not others. We would have treated him fairly. We understand about accidents. Why cannot they trust us?' said Mahmoud bitterly.

'They do trust you,' said Owen quickly. 'Of course they trust you!' It could come out of the blue, this touching of the Egyptian nerve.

'Even from their point of view it is a mistake. It makes you ask questions. It made *me* ask questions. When the Mudir couldn't answer them I went round to the Russian Consulate, because Tvardovsky was, after all, one of their nationals, but they – well, it wasn't as if they weren't interested, rather that they suddenly closed down. They wouldn't tell me anything. And then I went to the Khedive's office – the Khedive was the host, after all – and got the same response from them. They wouldn't even give me a list of who was there. And so I thought: why won't they? Is it that they have something to hide?'

They arrived at the hotel in late mid morning. It was beginning to get very hot and people were already returning from excursions along the bank of the lake. The hotel, which had been emptied of its guests to accommodate the Khedive's party was full again with its normal clientele: Greek and Levantine businessmen escaping the heat of the city with their families, old hands of the Administration who had done all the sights and were looking for something green, somewhere, perhaps, that would remind them of England, a few foreign tourists complete with Kodaks.

They went at once down to the lake. The foreshore was now lined with boats. Fishermen were shovelling their catch into wickerwork baskets. Every so often one of them would lift a basket on to his shoulder, step over the side of the boat and splash ashore. Gulls would swoop down even as he was carrying and snap at the fish. The baskets were taken to an outbuilding of the hotel, where the fish were emptied out on to the floor. Through the open door Owen could see the grey-and-silvery pile growing and growing.

The heaps of fish inside the boats were diminishing rapidly. From time to time one of the fish would give a squirm and a jump and then fall back again. Some of the fishermen had turned to coiling their ropes and spreading their nets out on the ground to dry.

Mahmoud went across and began to talk to some of them. They pointed along the bank to where the shoot had taken place. The reeds were thick at this point, about six feet high and spreading out in a little headland. The shoot had taken place just off the headland. Around the other side, where ducks crowded in such numbers as to make the water white.

Mahmoud climbed into one of the punt-like boats and two

of the boatmen prepared to paddle him over. He asked Owen to go with him.

The men had been on the shoot itself, in the boats where the bulk of the party had been stationed, in the open water beyond the headland, just at the edge of the reeds, where the reeds would conceal them. They were describing to Mahmoud what had happened, putting their arms up to mimic the shooting.

It hardly seemed possible it could be the same place. Then the air had been torn by shooting, there had been a kind of tension. Now everything seemed incredibly peaceful. Ducks were dawdling in and out of the reeds, hardly bothering to register their presence. The sun was warm on the woodwork, the blue lake sparkled in the sun, as still as a mirror. He found it hard to reconcile with his memory.

'Of course,' he said to Mahmoud, 'we weren't out there. We were in there.'

He pointed vaguely towards the reeds.

'We?' said Mahmoud.

'Tvardovsky and I. In two separate boats.'

'Just the two of you?'

'Yes.'

'Why was that?'

'We had different boats. They could go in among the reeds.'

'How did you come to have different boats?'

Owen shrugged.

'Accident. Maybe we arrived later than the others. The other boats were all taken.'

Mahmoud took the boat over to the reeds and peered in. They were impenetrable to a boat like his.

'How would you see to shoot?' he asked.

'You would be shooting upwards. You would see the birds against the sky.' He tried to remember. 'You wouldn't have long. Of course,' he added, 'Tvardovsky wasn't shooting.'

Mahmoud sat there for some time thinking. Then he told the boatmen to take the boat back to the land. There Owen saw him talking to the man who had been Tvardovsky's boatman.

He came back towards Owen.

'You were in a separate boat,' he said. 'Where is your boatman?'

Owen looked around and couldn't see him.

Mahmoud spoke to some of the men.

'He's gone to visit his mother,' he said.

The boats had finished emptying their catch now. The nets had been spread out along the bank. There was a stink of fish in the air. Some of the men had gone to sit in the shade of a large boat that had been drawn up out of the water. Mahmoud stayed talking to them for some time.

Owen wandered along the bank. He came to a small bay where flamingoes were paddling on the lake. Beside them was a pair of pelicans. As Owen watched, one of the pelicans stooped down into the water and came up with a fish. Owen saw its tail disappearing into the bird's beak as it was swallowed. It was a large fish and made a bulge in the pelican's neck. With horrified fascination Owen watched the bulge wriggling as it went down.

The Mudir was sitting under a palm tree chatting to some waiters. Mahmoud went across to greet him and then brought him back to a table on the terrace, where he summoned coffee. The Mudir sat down uneasily. While a Parquet officer did not count as the great, the Parquet itself was a mysterious object over the horizon from which from time to time incomprehensible reproofs would come like a bolt from the blue.

'The man was dead,' he said, shifting uncomfortably in his seat. 'What need of a postmortem?'

'To establish the cause of death.'

'He was shot. There is no puzzle about that.'

'Yes, but –'

'And, besides, he was a foreign effendi.'

'So?'

The Mudir shrugged.

'You don't mess about with foreign effendis,' he said, 'even when they're dead.'

'You have a responsibility,' said Mahmoud sternly, 'to establish how he died.'

'I know how he died! He was shot. There!' The Mudir clapped his chest dramatically.

'At what range?'

'What range?'

'How far away was the person who fired the shot?'

'Well, hell, I don't know. It was among the reeds and –'

'The postmortem might be able to tell you that.'

'But can't we guess? The shot must have been fired from one of the boats and –'

'The boats were scattered. I know, because I asked the boatmen. If we knew the range, it might help us to establish which boat.'

'Anyway,' said the Mudir lamely, 'there was no ice.'

'Ice? What's that got to do with it?'

'To pack the body in. If we wanted to preserve it for a postmortem. It's very hot at this time of year and –'

'But there was plenty of ice! The hotel had lots of it.'

'Ah, yes, but that was ice for putting in drinks. You couldn't use that. Not for a foreign effendi. It would be disrespectful.'

'So what did you do with the body?'

'I let the effendis have it.'

'You *what*?'

'I let the effendis take it away. They said they would see to all that was necessary. And I said to myself, yes, surely that would be best, for they will know what is proper. Who am I to say what rites should be used for a foreign effendi? You can't expect a Mudir to know everything.'

'You let them take it away? Just like that? Without even getting a doctor to sign a death certificate? Have you no notion of procedure, man?'

'It wasn't like that,' protested the Mudir, stung. 'These were foreign effendis, great and mighty. And, besides, Prince

27

Fuad said if I didn't get a move on, he would kick my arse.'

'There is a procedure to be followed,' lectured Mahmoud, 'and you, the Mudir, should be seeing that it *is* followed. No one is above the law. Neither foreign effendis nor Prince Fuad.'

'You try telling Prince Fuad that!' said the Mudir.

3

The tables on the terrace were filling up now for lunch. White tablecloths gleamed, silver serviette rings shone. Ice buckets smoked, ice chinked in glasses. Mahmoud had gone into the hotel to see if he could obtain a list of the people who had been there on the weekend when Tvardovsky was shot. Owen was reading the wine list.

A man came out on to the terrace. He stopped when he saw Owen and then came across to him.

'Why, Captain Owen,' he said, 'what brings you here? Taking a break? Oh, no,' he smiled, 'I was forgetting: you will be here on business. This sad Tvardovsky affair!'

Owen did not recognize him.

'Mirza es-Rahel,' said the man helpfully. 'I work for *Al-Liwa*.'

'I know your writing, of course,' said Owen, 'but the face –'

They shook hands. It was true. He did know his writings. And very scurrilous they were, too. The man seemed to have a knack of unearthing scandalous stories about the royal family and the politicians with whom the Khedive surrounded himself. But the face was unfamiliar.

Which was surprising, for Owen thought he knew most of the important Nationalist journalists who worked in the city.

'I'm based in Alexandria,' the Egyptian explained.

That, too, was surprising: for it was Cairo that was the hub of government, the place where the Khedive and his ministers resided, and where one would naturally expect to find journalists of Mr es-Rahel's ilk. He said as much.

'But it is Alexandria where the money is,' said the Egyptian, smiling again, 'and I have always found the financial connection the most promising of threads to pursue.'

'Not sex?'

'That, too,' Mr es-Rahel conceded. 'But sex is for pleasure: money is something you take seriously.' He laughed. 'Or, at least, the Pashas who rule us do.'

'And which is it that brings you here, Mr es-Rahel? Business or pleasure?'

'Pleasure. Though not, I'm afraid, of the sexual kind. Merely taking a break. I was feeling a bit jaded. Alexandria, you know, fills up at this time of year with holiday-makers. I felt a day or two in the quiet by the lake would do me good.' He looked across to the main building and saw Mahmoud coming out of a door. 'You are here with Mr El Zaki?'

'Yes.'

'Seeing that he does not find out too much?'

The conciliating laugh took the sting out of his words.

'Helping him.'

'I am sure he will need help. With so many obstacles in his way.'

'Are there?'

'Well, yes, Captain Owen. You know that as well as I do.'

'What sort of obstacles?'

'The usual ones. The ones that always block Egypt's attempts at freedom.'

'The Capitulations, you mean?'

'Exactly.'

'I am not sure they are relevant here.'

'No?'

'In any case,' said Owen, 'there's not a lot I can do about them.'

'Perhaps not. But, you see, Captain Owen, if you were really helping Mr El-Zaki, it would make his task a great deal easier. That is why I asked what was your role in the case.'

'Why are you interested in Tvardovsky?'

The journalist spread his hands.

'The general good, Captain Owen. The general good. This is a sad loss to Egypt.'

'A sad loss?'

Es-Rahel caught the note of incredulity and stared.

'Why, yes, Captain Owen. Mr Tvardovsky was a man who might have done a great deal for Egypt.'

'That was the point of the gathering, certainly.'

'Ah, yes, but you know how these things go. So many people there who were not really interested in Egypt, interested only in how much money they could make out of it. Mr Tvardovsky was not like that.'

'You knew Tvardovsky?'

'Of course.'

'Of course?'

'We journalists mix in a variety of circles.'

'Including that of millionaire financiers?'

'Well, perhaps not directly,' the Egyptian admitted. 'But we do sometimes meet them in other circles.'

'Such as?'

'Émigré ones.' Mr es-Rahel smiled. 'Radical ones, Captain Owen. But then, the Mamur Zapt wouldn't know about that sort of circle, would he?'

Mahmoud joined them.

'Ah, Mr El-Zaki!' said the journalist warmly. 'And how are you getting on with your inquiries? Successfully, I hope. Mr Tvardovsky was such a sad loss to us all!'

Mahmoud looked at him distrustfully.

'Mirza es-Rahel,' said the journalist, shaking hands.

'He works for *Al-Liwa*,' said Owen.

'Oh.'

Mahmoud was not on easy terms with the press. Partly it was his natural caution. As a Parquet lawyer, Mahmoud had had too much experience of journalists not to know that anything he said would be taken down and used in evidence against him. But partly, too, it was a slightly puritanical dislike of their overstatement and distortion. Why couldn't they just put it down straightforwardly and rationally – like a law report, for instance?

'I was just urging Captain Owen to give you all the help he could,' said es-Rahel.

'Oh, yes?' said Mahmoud distantly.

'I am afraid you will need it,' said the journalist, 'with all there is ranged against you.'

'Oh, yes?'

'You can, of course, count on our support. But in a case like this the Mamur Zapt's support, if indeed, you have it, will count far more.'

'Well, thank you,' said Mahmoud.

For Mahmoud, as for most Cairenes, Africa began one mile south of Cairo. In the wilderness that was the provinces, what hope was there for observance of proper procedure? For efficiency and competence of any sort? For rationality itself?

'Be fair!' remonstrated Owen. 'He's only a Mudir. And when he's up against someone like Prince Fuad –'

'That is true. It is wrong for me to blame the ones lower down when it is those at the top who are at fault. What you said is true. It is not the Mudir who is to blame, it is those who have made him what he is!'

He brought his fist crashing down on the table. A waiter, misunderstanding, hurried to replenish their coffee pot.

'It is not the man who is at fault, it is the system. The Pashas, with their interest in keeping people ignorant, the Khedive, the British –'

'Quite right!' said the waiter warmly.

'What?'

Caught off balance, Mahmoud stared up at him.

'It's what I always say myself.'

It was the waiter that Owen knew, the one he had had his long conversation with on the occasion of his previous visit to the hotel, that morning when the financiers had been talking under the trees and he himself had been sitting, then as now, up here on the terrace.

'It's the rich man that gets syrup on his figs, the poor man has to do without.'

He poured them some coffee.

'Take this coffee, for instance. Do you think I get coffee like this? Well, I do, as a matter of fact, because I work in the hotel now and we help ourselves. But when I'm at home, do you think I drink like this? No, it's bitter black tea for me, and that's the way it is with the world. The rich get what's going and the poor are left to fend for themselves.'

'Yes, well –'

The waiter dropped on to his heels, part of the conversation now.

'Take that foreign effendi, the one who was shot. Did the Mudir want to know? Not a bit of it. In fact, the less he knew about it, the better. But when my sister's son was caught stealing grapes, the Mudir was on to him in a flash. "It's you for the caracol," he said. Caracol! What did he want to put him in the caracal for, for a thing like that? A clip over the ear would have done. Or a touch of the stick, like the old Mudir used to do. "You're making him a criminal," I said. "I'm bloody stopping him from becoming one," the Mudir says. Well, that's all very well, but what about those rich men who were here the other day? They were stealing grapes if anyone was. But was anybody doing anything about them? Well, maybe someone was, for one of them got shot, didn't he? Though he was the wrong man and they should have shot someone else –'

'Just a minute,' interrupted Owen: 'Why? Why was he the wrong man?'

'Well, he was all right, wasn't he? A bit lacking in the brain-pan, perhaps, the way he talked sometimes and the way he poked around in places, but harmless. You could see he meant well. When he went into shops or the bazaar he used to talk to people –'

'Shops?' said Owen. 'Bazaar? Where was this?'

'Medinet. He used to go there regularly. There was an old woman he used to stay with. As batty as he was. Foreign, of course, like him. Well, you can't get away from them, they're everywhere in Egypt. But –'

'He'd been here before?'

'Not here. Medinet. And over at Lahoun. He was always over there at the Labyrinth. Wouldn't have been surprised if a crocodile had had him one of these days, if half what they say is true.'

'What do they say?'

'They say they haven't gone, you know.'

'They –?'

'The crocodiles. They say they're still there somewhere. Tucked away underground in that Labyrinth. And they'll have you as soon as look at you if you don't watch out. People wandering around on their own. Like him. Tempting fate. Though fate's a funny thing, isn't it? It wasn't the crocodiles that got him in the end. Although what happened to the body? They say that daft Mudir gave it away. You can never be sure about these things. Maybe the crocodiles did get him after all. A pity, though, it was him and not one of the others. Everybody knew him and –'

'Everybody knew him?' said Mahmoud later, as they climbed up into the carriage that was taking them back to the train.

Medinet spread along both banks of the Bahr-el-Yussuf. If it was a canal, as some argued, it was an unusual one, for the water rushed along it as swiftly as in a river. The current was so powerful that the water-wheels which fed the town were worked directly by it. The houses, too, were interesting, many of them as grand as Cairo Mameluke houses, with stuccoed fronts and graceful balconies trailing roses and figs and vines.

The house they were looking for was one of these, fronting, or possibly backing, on to the Bahr-el-Yussuf itself. While the porter went off to find out if the Sitt would see them, they waited in a mandar'ah, or reception room, which had a sunken, tessellated floor and a dais at one end with large worn cushions on which they could sit.

They were taken, though, to the takhtabosh, which was a kind of recess off the small central courtyard, with an open front and a single column supporting a central arch. There was an open gateway on to the river and the takhtabosh was situated so that it would catch something of the river breeze.

The Sitt was an old frail lady, who received them with the manner of a *grande dame* of the previous century, an impression deepened by the fact that she addressed them in French. It was not the French of France, however, nor even the French of Egypt.

'No,' she said. 'I come from Russia. We came here many years ago when my husband' – the voice faltered a little – 'had to leave Russia. It was after Alexander came to the throne. My husband's family was not popular with the Romanovs. It never had been. One of his forebears took part in the Dekembrist insurrection, a fact of which' – she lifted her head and looked them straight in the eyes – 'I am very proud. Anyway, he had to leave Russia. He set up a business in Alexandria, importing and exporting, and we lived there until he retired. He had always loved this part of Egypt, the water, the birds, the roses, and so we bought this house. And I have lived here ever since.'

'You kept in touch, however, with some Russian friends, Tvardovsky –'

'Ah, yes,' she said, 'poor Tvardovsky! He always came to see me when he was in Alexandria on business. He made a point of it. He said our house was full of beautiful things. Come,' she said, 'I will show you them.'

She stood up, with difficulty, and, supporting herself on a stick, led them through the house: into the mak'ad, the high central hall, with its decorated ceiling and its kamarija windows, consisting of tiny pieces of coloured glass set in panels of pierced plaster taking the shapes of arabesques or flowers, or even a phoenix, which threw a brilliantly coloured reflection on the ground; up into the old harem, with its box-like meshrebiya windows; down into the ka'ah, with its inlaid cupboards and irregular recesses for holding china.

They did hold china: lots of it. Everywhere there were beautiful bowls and vases, huge, richly decorated plates, some from the time of the Mameluke Sultans, others even older. From classical Greece, perhaps?

'Oh, no! Here. The Fayoum. Not Greek Greek but Egyptian Greek. The Fayoum is a treasure trove of such things and these are some of its treasures.'

They went into another room with a sunken floor and a fountain playing in the middle of it. A wooden mastaba, or bench, ran along one wall. Leaning against the opposite wall, so that you could sit on the mastaba and study them, were some wooden panels with faces painted on them.

'Mummy portraits,' said the old lady. 'The panels were inserted over the mummy wrappings. The portrait was a likeness of the dead person.'

'Where do they come from?'

'Near here. Over at Hawara. There was an archaeologist working there. His name was Petrie. He often used to stay at our house and my husband got to know him well. The best ones have gone to museums, but there were some that were damaged or even in pieces. He let us have some of those and my husband had them made good. If you look carefully you can see the joins. But if you are looking that carefully you can also see beyond the joins to what was there in the first place. And what was there was, well – you can see for yourselves.'

The faces seemed to leap out at you. They hadn't the stylized, dead look of much classical portraiture but were individual, strong, vivid, as if their subjects might have started up a conversation with you at any moment. The eyes were large and rounded, the eyebrows arched. The hair was short and curly. They were the sort of faces that you might see today at any Mediterranean resort.

36

'Encaustic on limewood. Some are tempera. I prefer the encaustic. The colours are richer. But what is so nice is that it's a mixture. Just like Egypt. This one, for instance. It's obviously Greek in its treatment of the face and the way it poses the figure. But the hairstyle and the jewellery are pure Rome.' She bent and peered at it. 'Mid-Antonine, I would say. But the context, the atmosphere – surely, entirely Egyptian!'

She stepped back.

'My husband loved them. And so did Tvardovsky. He used to sit here for hours looking at them. Funny, that – that he, the son of a serf –'

She looked at them.

'Did you know that? His father was a serf on our estate. My father freed him when the Emancipation Act went through. He still went on working on the estate, though, and Tvardovsky grew up there. My father paid to have him educated – he was always very clever, you could see it from the start. When he left school he worked for us for a time, not in the fields – that would have been a waste – but in the office. He was often in the house and I think it was there that he acquired his love of beautiful things. My mother used to take him round and tell him about them. Of course, he didn't stay with us for long. He went away and became rich, and we –'

She laughed.

'Well, I married Boris. He didn't exactly become poor but he had to leave Russia in a hurry. We lost touch with Tvardovsky but then, years later, he found us again.'

She shook her head.

'Poor Tvardovsky! He was a lovely man.'

'We are investigating his death.'

'And so you should!'

'It may, of course, have been an accident.'

'It was no accident,' she said firmly.

'You say that very definitely.'

'I feel it in my bones.'

'But is there any other reason? Had he enemies?'

37

'For anyone in Russia interested in democracy,' she said, 'there is always one enemy: the Tsar.'

Among the stalls selling such things as onions, sugar cane and poultry (live) which made up the bazaar at Medinet, Tvardovsky was, as the waiter at the hotel had said, well known; but the most useful information came from the barber, holding court under the trees behind them, his bowls and instruments spread on the ground beside him, his victim sitting apprehensively on a dilapidated, wickerwork chair, and an admiring circle of supporters squatted round. The man to talk to, he said, was the Sheikh of the madrissa.

'Sheikh' was an honorary title given to religious leaders. The school, however, was not one of the traditional ones, where only the Koran was taught, but one of the new government ones which had a wider range of subjects. The respect that the title suggested became understandable at once when they rounded a corner and saw two boys ahead of them dressed in Eton jackets and turn-down collars.

'This is what English boys wear?' asked Mahmoud, impressed.

'Not where I was,' said Owen.

The madrissa, they said, was on the edge of the town. It had closed now for the day but the Sheikh would still be there, outside on a bed, resting. They offered to show the way.

As they walked along, one of the boys said to Owen: 'I know you.'

'I don't think you do,' said Owen.

'You are the Mamur Zapt.'

'How did you know that?' asked Owen, astonished.

'My uncle is a waiter at the hotel where the effendi was shot and he told me that there was one there who stayed behind afterwards and was the Mamur Zapt.'

'Even so, how –?'

The boy put on an imitation of what even Owen could see was an Englishman, although he could not see how it applied to himself.

Mahmoud laughed.

'Wait a minute,' said Owen, 'then you must be the boy who was stealing grapes?'

'It's a lie!' said the boy. 'They fell off by themselves. I found them in the road.'

'I thought you were put in the caracol?'

'The Sheikh spoke for me.'

'It is bad,' remonstrated Mahmoud, 'that a boy like you, who is evidently high in the Sheikh's esteem, should be found doing a thing like that.'

'Well, I wouldn't have been found if the ghaffir had not crept up behind the wall. And he certainly wouldn't have caught me had it not been for the fiki.'

'Fiki?'

'He came up the other way through the bushes and when I lingered to exchange words with the ghaffir –'

'The ghaffir should have been treated with respect!'

'He is old and fat.'

'Even so. He was but doing his duty.'

'He does his duty when it comes to boys and grapes. But grapes are a small thing. What when it comes to big things? Then he sits on his big fat behind and does nothing. He is not like the Sheikh, who speaks the same words to big as to small.'

'You think well of the Sheikh, then?'

'When the man comes from the Ministry, I will speak up for him.'

'That, I am sure, he will be grateful for.'

The boy gave him a sideways look.

'It is not a small thing. The Sheikh's dues depend on the man from the Ministry. But when he questions the others, they will not speak up. But I will speak up. I will give the right answers and then the man from the Ministry will know that our Sheikh is a good Sheikh.'

'That is highly laudable. Be sure, though, that they *are* the right answers.'

'There will be no problem about that; for I am at the head

39

of my class. The Sheikh says that great things lie ahead of me. If I do not steal grapes.'

They walked on a little way in silence. Then the boy said: 'I am going to be a lawyer when I grow up.'

'My friend is a lawyer,' said Owen, indicating Mahmoud. 'He is from the Parquet.'

The boy looked troubled.

'It was only grapes,' he said defensively.

A man was lying on a rope bed, his bare feet open to the air.

'Ya Sheikh,' called the boy. 'Effendis are here to see you.'

The man sprang up, thrust his feet into shoes, seized a jacket and hurried out to meet them.

'Your pardon!' he said. 'I was just taking a rest after teaching.'

'It is we who need pardon,' said Mahmoud courteously, 'for disturbing you.'

'Please, please!'

The man led them into the building.

'You have come to see the school?' he said hopefully.

'That, we would like to,' said Mahmoud, 'if time permits. However, our main business is that we wish to talk to you.'

'You are from the Ministry?'

'I am from the Parquet.'

'The Parquet?' said the headmaster puzzled.

'People have told us that you knew Tvardovsky.'

'Ah, Tvardovsky.'

The man's face clouded over.

'Poor Tvardovsky,' he said quietly. 'Yes, I knew him.'

He led them along a corridor, past classrooms with picture cards and maps on the walls, and into his office, a little, bare room, scattered, however, with shards of pottery, and with pots in various stages of reconstruction.

'Tvardovsky was interested in this,' he said, seeing their glance. 'That is what brought us together.'

'You knew him well?'

40

'He came to see me every time he was over here. We used to go over to Lahoun and to Hawara. I was his guide. I knew the places well,' he explained, 'because I was always going over there. It is my hobby. As you see,' he said, with a gesture of his hand.

'Could you take us there?'

'It would need donkeys. And at this time in the afternoon –'

'There is no problem,' said a voice from the door. 'I will supply.'

'Ibrahim –'

But the boy had already vanished.

The headmaster sighed.

'He is a good boy. But –'

'He likes grapes.'

The Sheikh laughed.

'While we are waiting,' he said, 'let me show you the school. It is one of the new government ones and we are very proud of it.'

He took them through some of the rooms. To Mahmoud, used to Egyptian classrooms, they seemed astonishingly well-equipped.

'It was Tvardovsky. He gave us the money. He always used to visit the school when he came. He said that this was where New Egypt started.'

'He did?' said Mahmoud.

'Yes. He used to say that this was the seed-corn; and that if it was to grow, three things were necessary, as with any enterprise: the right man, resources, and the vision. He said' – the headmaster gestured in self-deprecation – 'that I was the right man and that he would supply the resources. As for the vision –'

The donkeys plodded slowly across the desert, urged by Ibrahim and a host of small boys. On this side of the town green had given way to brown.

'It wasn't always like this,' said the headmaster. 'In the days when Lake Karoun was Lake Moeris, the water stretched right up to Hawara. It was an artificial lake, of course. The regulator was at Lahoun. You can still see the remains of the dykes and the sluices.'

He took them there, since that, he said, was where Tvardovsky liked to go.

'He used to say: if man could do this four thousand six hundred years ago, why cannot he do it now? I would say, the land has changed since that time. No, no, he would say, it is not the land that has changed, but man. Man changes the land. And then he would tramp all over the place and he would show me how it could be done.'

The headmaster smiled.

'I do not know if he was right,' he confessed. 'It seemed far-fetched to me. But then,' he said sadly, 'Tvardovsky was the one with the vision.'

Across the desert they could see the Lahoun Brick Pyramid and then, as they swung round to go back to Medinet, the Great Pyramid at Hawara.

'Tvardovsky was always here,' said the headmaster, 'especially when the Germans were excavating the mummy cemetery. He was as excited as a child. "What things they are finding," he used to say, "what things!"'

'Did Tvardovsky collect himself?' asked Owen.

'No, I don't think so. He lived, so he told me, like a Bedouin on the march, always on the move, so he had no place to put them. He just liked seeing them. I think it was part of his dream, really. He looked around and he saw the place as it had been and as it might be. Under the Ptolemies it was one of the most important centres in Egypt. Even before that, under the Pharaohs –'

He pointed across the desert.

'Over there is the Labyrinth. At least, that's what they call it. In fact, latest opinion is that it's nothing of the kind but the place where a national assembly used to meet. Like,' he said to Owen, 'your House of Commons. It was vast – twelve separate courtyards, over three thousand rooms – and some say it was too big to be just an assembly hall and that it was probably government offices. Tvardovsky liked that. He said it was far more probable that it was given over to bureaucracy than to democracy.'

The headmaster smiled, remembering.

'He used to say, though, that the name "Labyrinth" might well still be right – that if these were government offices then there probably *was* a monster in them somewhere.'

Just before sunset they reached the edge of Medinet. The headmaster, however, did not lead them straight back into the town but off to one side, to a place where the ground was broken by lots of little humps and where the sand crackled under the donkeys' feet. Looking down, Owen saw that the ground was littered with hundreds and hundreds of broken pot shards.

'Arsinoe,' said the headmaster, 'the town the Greeks called Crocodilopolis. The water once came right up to here. The Ministers probably had their houses along the edge of the lake. Tvardovsky used to say this must have been where they played their power games; so that the losers could be disposed of conveniently to the crocodiles. Just like, he said, Cairo.'

4

'The body?' said the man at the Consulate blankly when they went to see him next day.

'Yes,' said Mahmoud patiently. 'I understand it was handed over to you.'

The man hunted through the papers.

'Oh, yes,' he said. 'The least we could do.'

'So what happened to it?'

'It was cremated. There was no point in repatriating it. It appears that he had no family in Russia. And, besides, the deterioration –'

'Is there a doctor's certificate?'

The man searched through the papers.

'There does not appear to be.'

'There should be. It is a requirement of the law that a body cannot be disposed of, whether by burial or cremation, without a doctor's certificate having been procured first.'

'Really? Well, I'm sure we did all we should. Perhaps back in the Fayoum –'

'But you know that cannot have been so. The body was handed over to you immediately –'

'Was it? Then it should not have been. Not without a doctor's certificate. There was obviously a slip-up. These provincial authorities –'

Mahmoud fought to keep hold of his temper.

'Were there any personal effects?'

'I believe so.'

'What happened to them? Cremated, too?'

44

The man smiled wintrily.

'What will happen to them has still to be resolved.'

'Was there a will?'

'Will? I don't think so. Perhaps there was. It will be something his lawyers might know.'

'Who are his lawyers?'

'Demetriades and Atiyah. At least, they're the ones who seem to have acted for him most. They have offices in Alexandria.'

'Have they been notified?'

'Of course. You can be sure,' said the man from the Consulate, smiling, 'that we have done everything that was necessary.'

'A very sad case,' said the lawyer to Owen the next day. 'Very sad indeed.'

'Sad for Egypt,' supplemented his partner, Atiyah. 'Tvardovsky was a man of imagination.'

'He could have done much for Egypt,' concurred Demetriades.

'Other countries, too,' said Atiyah. 'He had interests throughout the Levant.'

'If only his projects had come off.'

'Well, some did, didn't they?' said Atiyah.

'They did. And so they might have done in Egypt,' said Demetriades. 'It was a great pity, as I said.'

'You have a picture of his interests?'

'Some of them. He used different lawyers for different fields.'

'He was interested in so many things,' said Demetriades.

'He was a man of great imagination,' said Atiyah admiringly.

'When will you have a complete picture of your side?' asked Owen.

'Oh, months,' said Demetriades.

'If not longer,' said Atiyah.

'His affairs are very complex.'

'Brilliant,' said Atiyah. 'He was technically very brilliant.'

'Unfortunately, that makes it very difficult to unravel them.'

45

'Did he leave a will?'

'Yes.'

'Could I see it?'

'Certainly. It is with Probate. We could have a copy made for you if you wished.'

'Please.'

'I will send a man down at once. The copy will be ready for you this afternoon.'

'Thank you.'

'Did he leave anything else?' said Owen. 'Were there any effects?'

'A few. He travelled very lightly.'

'What did they consist of?'

'What was left in his *appartement*.' Demetriades glanced at Atiyah. Atiyah nodded. 'You may wish to see his *appartement*.'

The *appartement* was on the top floor of a residential block. Its vast bay window faced out over the sea. There were two bedrooms as well as the living room, and, of course, a kitchen and bathroom.

For a moment Owen could not take it in. The *appartement* had been very thoroughly searched. 'Searched' was, perhaps, not the word. 'Devastated' would have been better. Drawers had been emptied out on to the floor, the doors of a cupboard had been forced open and the fine china-ware inside pulled impatiently out on to the carpet. Cushions had been ripped open. Even the divan had been slit and searched.

They walked through into the bedrooms. It was the same story there. The mattresses had been tipped off the beds. The doors of the single wardrobe were hanging open, Tvardovsky's suits and ties spilling out on to the carpet. The drawers of his dressing table were sagging down, brushes, cufflink boxes, bow ties thrown hurriedly out, littering the floor beneath.

The kitchen had been treated in the same way. Pots and pans were scattered about the floor. Cutlery was lying everywhere. Even the large earthenware pot which held his bread had been tipped over.

They went back into the living room. Owen saw now that
the walls had been hung with fine carpets in the Arab style,
which had all been torn down and were lying at the foot of the
walls. Whoever had searched had looked as well for a safe.

Tvardovsky had had one or two pictures which had suffered
the same fate. They were lying on the floor, their glass shat-
tered. One of them had slipped down behind the divan. He
went across and picked it up. It was a mummy portrait such
as he had seen in the old lady's house in the Fayoum. There
was no glass here; just the face itself, painted on wood.

Mahmoud stood in the middle of the carpet looking round.

'Who did this?' he said.

Demetriades shrugged.

'You should see his office,' he said.

The office was down by the docks in one of the roads running
back from the sea. At the lower end, nearer the wharves,
there were ships' chandlers, rope-sellers, oil-sellers and shops
selling instruments whose purpose Owen did not recognize
but which were something presumably to do with the sea.
Higher up, the road broadened out and there were trees.
The shops gave way to offices: moneylenders, pawnbrokers,
the occasional lawyer and doctor, ships' agents. At the top
end was an office marked simply 'Tvardovsky'. Its door was
heavily padlocked.

Demetriades glanced at Atiyah. Atiyah nodded.

'There is another door,' said Demetriades. 'The key is with
Tvardovsky's man.'

He took them through the narrow side streets until they
came to some steps leading down to a basement. The door
at the bottom was open. Demetriades went to it and called:

'You, Daniel! Ya, Daniel!'

An old woman came slowly to the door.

'Who is it?' she said.

'It is Demetriades; with some friends.'

'Demetriades can come in. Who are the friends?'

'The Parquet.'

'The Parquet will come in,' said the old woman, 'whether one wishes it or not.'

The door gave on to a large, dark, cool room in which a man was lying on a divan. He started to get up.

'Be still, Daniel,' said Demetriades. 'We come only for the key.'

'With the key,' said Daniel, 'comes the man who guards it.'

He came with them, painfully slowly, to the office.

'You worked for Tvardovsky, friend?' said Mahmoud courteously.

'I did. Here, as in Istanbul.'

'That was before he came here?'

'I have worked with him ever since he came out here. When first he set up office he sent for me and said: "I want you to work with me." I said: "I do not like Russians." "Why is that?" he said. "Because I am a Russian," I said, "and because of what they did to me." "I need you," he said. Well, at that time I needed him, for there was no work for Jews in Istanbul. So I began to work in his office, and have done his business ever since.'

'What was his business?'

'He lent money to people who wished to build or expand their affairs. Only to people like that. He lent only for business. He liked to see businesses grow, he said. For in that way prosperity was spread. And as with a man, so with a country. He liked to see countries grow. He wished,' said the old man, 'to see Egypt grow.'

'And so he went to the Fayoum?'

'The Fayoum was close to his heart. He believed he could restore it to what it had been, when Egypt's crops were so great that their abundance spilled over even to Rome. He talked to everyone about it but no one would listen. That was why he went to the lake that day. "This thing is too big for me alone," he said. "There must be others." He hoped to persuade them. He went to the Khedive's Minister and said: "Let me come; for I know what can be done." But the Minister said: "This is for Russians only." "But I *am* a Russian!" said Tvardovsky. "Ask the Russians, then," said the Minister.

'So Tvardovsky went to the Russian Consul and said: "I want to be put on your list." But at first they would not, for they did not like him. However, he pressed and pressed and in the end they said: "Well, why not?" That day when he came back to the office, he was like a child, beside himself with joy. It was only after that –'

'That what?'

'He changed. It happened suddenly. One day he came into the office and sat at his desk and I could see that he was disturbed. "What is the matter?" I said. "Nothing is the matter," he said. But from that day he was somehow different. I could tell that he was worried, and I said: "Do not go, then." But he said: "I must go. For this is my chance." I thought that it would pass, that, perhaps, this being a big thing for him, he was merely nervous. But as the day came closer –'

'Yes?'

'I could see that he was not nervous but frightened.'

The door was up a dark alleyway at the rear of the house which the rubbish men used to collect the litter. Not too successfully; the ground was strewn with refuse of all kinds, some vegetable, some animal. Demetriades glanced at them apologetically.

'It is used by all the inhabitants of the block,' he said. 'And by some who are not inhabitants.'

Including, it would seem, the dogs of the neighbourhood.

They wiped their feet as they went in. The door led into a corridor. Three rooms opened off it, one used as a storeroom, the other two as offices. All three had been taken apart. Filing cabinets were sagging open, their contents spilled out all over the floor. Desk drawers had simply been pulled out and tipped on to the desk tops. Box files standing on shelves had been swept off and broken open. An old padded chair had had its seat ripped. They had even felt inside.

In the storeroom old files had been pulled out and then

thrown on the floor. Some package chests in one corner had been broken open. A tin box had had its lock forced off.

'Who did this?' said Mahmoud.

'The police,' said the old man.

'Like this?' said Owen. He couldn't believe it.

'Even if it was the police,' said Mahmoud, 'they must have been under someone.' His lips went thin. 'It could not have been the Parquet.'

'Perhaps it was the Secret Police?' suggested the old man.

'Nonsense!' said Owen. The only Secret Police in Egypt were his.

The old man shrugged.

'When was this done?' asked Mahmoud.

'We found it like this,' said Demetriades. 'When we came here. After the Consulate had notified us.'

'It was the same day,' said the old man. 'When I came in the morning it was like this. You came here in the afternoon.'

'Did you notify the police?' Mahmoud asked him.

The old man smiled.

'What's the use?' he said.

'Was anything taken?' asked Owen.

'It is hard to tell,' said the old man, 'but I do not think so.'

'Papers?'

'I would have to go through them. But what I can tell you is that if they were looking for anything important, they would not have found it. Tvardovsky kept everything in his head.'

'Surely not everything?'

'The most important things: his plans.'

'That is true,' said Demetriades. 'He committed little to paper.'

'But I saw him with papers!' said Owen. 'That night in the tent.'

'They must have been other people's papers, then.'

Mahmoud looked round the room.

'Cash?'

'He put it straight in the bank.'

50

'Which bank was that?'

'The British Bank of the Levant. It was the only one he trusted. It is British, he said, and they allow no one to rob but themselves.'

Owen found he knew the manager of the bank. It was Jarvis, the Chairman of the British Chamber of Commerce, whom he had seen at the conference in the Fayoum.

'Tvardovsky?' Jarvis said, without enthusiasm. 'Well, we knew him, of course. He was always in and out. But I can't say we knew him well. He was always' – he hesitated – 'a bit odd.' He shot a quick glance at Owen. 'Ran a home for seamen,' he said.

'Tvardovsky?' said Owen, astonished.

The manager nodded.

'Down on the docks,' he said. 'Well,' he amended, 'perhaps not actually ran it, but he had a lot to do with it. Had his office down there, too, not up here where you would expect. Well, I mean, it makes a difference. If you're always running into a chap, you get to know him. But if he's always hanging about with a bunch of layabouts and troublemakers –'

'Seamen, you mean?'

'That's right. It's no wonder the banking community found him a bit awkward.'

'Awkward? In what respect?'

'Take this De Vries and Boutigny business.'

'De Vries and Boutigny?' said Owen cautiously.

'It's a recent ruling of the Court of First Instance. There's been a big to-do about it. I expect you've heard?'

'Not sure I quite recall the details –'

'Well, it declared that the City and Agricultural Land of Egypt, Ltd – a perfectly respectable company, mind you – was null and nonexistent!'

'Good heavens!'

'Not only that,' said Jarvis, gratified. 'It went on to declare that all companies, *all* companies, mark you, similarly constituted, whose business was exclusively in Egypt and whose

51

board meetings were held in Egypt, were also null and nonexistent!'

'Is that so?' gasped Owen, not having the foggiest.

'Yes. Unbelievable, isn't it? I don't mind telling you that when I heard about it, I blew my top. Do you realize, I said to the Governor, the effect this could have? It could wipe out half the economy!'

'My goodness!'

'Yes. Something to think about, isn't it? "Is that what you want," I said? "To wipe us out?" "The law's the law," he said. "Well, yes," I said, "I know that. But if it's going to do things like this, you'd better see about changing it." I mean, who runs this bloody country, us or the lawyers?'

'I'm sorry,' said Owen, 'but I'm afraid I still don't see quite what the point at issue is.'

'Well, the Mixed Tribunals are claiming that companies like that are formed under foreign law specifically so that they can evade Egyptian company law. Foreign law, I said? But it's not foreign law, it's set up under English law. And if that's not good enough for a place like this, I'd like to know what is?'

'Quite so. However –'

'I don't mind telling you I was stunned when I heard about it. Devastated! "It's outrageous!" I said to the Governor. "It'll go to Appeal," he said. "Yes, I know," I said, "but who will it go on Appeal *to*? Bloody lawyers, again!" The whole business community was up in arms about it, I can tell you. Except Tvardovsky.'

'Not Tvardovsky?'

'No. He said it seemed to him quite reasonable. "You don't know what side your bread is buttered on, my man," I said. He just laughed. He said that sounded very English. But what if you didn't have any butter to put on your bread?'

The seamen's home was on the corner of the street. It was a long, low building which had perhaps once been a restaurant, for a stone mastaba ran along the front. The room they stepped down into, too, was underground. There were several men in it sitting at low tables. In a corner some Arabs were smoking from water-pipes, the little gourds on the ground beside them. There was a sweet smell in the air.

A man rose and came towards them.

'Effendis?'

'Parquet,' said Mahmoud.

The man's smile disappeared.

'What is it this time?'

'This time?'

'You are always here.'

Mahmoud sniffed the air.

'What do you expect?' he said.

'It wasn't that,' said the man.

'We want to talk about Tvardovsky,' said Owen.

'Again?'

'I don't understand,' said Mahmoud. 'This is the first time the Parquet has been here.'

The man shrugged.

'Someone else, then?'

'It matters,' said Owen. 'We want to find out how Tvardovsky died.'

'Why don't you ask them?'

However, he led them to a table and indicated that they should sit down. A waiter in a dirty galabeah brought coffee. The men at the next table got up and left.

'Strakhov isn't here,' said the man. 'They came and took him away.'

'Who is Strakhov?'

The man looked at them in surprise.

'He runs this place.'

'Not you, then?'

'I just help.'

'And Tvardovsky?'

'Tvardovsky provided the money.'

'Why did he do that? Why was he interested in a place like this?'

53

'It was the kind of thing Tvardovsky did,' said the man quietly.

'But why seamen especially? Had he been one himself?'

'Tvardovsky?' The man laughed. 'Perhaps it was the connection with Strakhov,' he said, however, after a moment.

'What was the connection?'

The man hesitated, then pointed to a door. To it was attached a notice which said: Russian Union of Seamen.

'Tvardovsky was in the union?'

'No, no. He was – sympathetic.'

Mahmoud got up and went over to the door. It was locked.

'They locked it when they took Strakhov away,' said the man.

'When was this?'

'Soon after Tvardovsky died.'

'Why was he taken away? On what grounds?'

The man shrugged.

'I don't know,' he said. 'You'd better ask them.'

Owen and Mahmoud exchanged glances. Mahmoud came back and sat down.

'Tell us about Strakhov,' he said.

'He was one of those who organized the Russian sailors' strike of 1906. They broke the strike and then they tried to break the union. The organizers were arrested but Strakhov got away. He was smuggled on to a boat and escaped to Alexandria. Tvardovsky got to know him somehow and tried to help him. He gave him the money to set up this home. He may have helped him set up the journal, too.'

'What journal was this?'

'It's called the *Moryak*, the *Sailor*. Well, then the union got in touch with him. They wanted to re-form. So, well, he set up a base for them here.'

'With money from Tvardovsky?'

The man hesitated.

'I don't know,' he said. 'I don't know how far Tvardovsky's support went.'

'You're a member of the union yourself?'

The man hesitated again.

'It doesn't matter,' said Mahmoud.

The man showed them out. As they went through the door, he said:

'It didn't take them long, did it? Once Tvardovsky was out of the way.'

'To do what?'

'Shut us down.'

'In Egypt,' said Mahmoud, 'we don't shut unions down.'

'No?' said the man.

'Who are "they"?' said Mahmoud, when they got outside.

'It must be the police. I'll have a word with the Commandant.'

'And meanwhile I'll have a word with the local Parquet,' said Mahmoud, 'just to make sure. And I'll try to find out about Strakhov.'

'Don't ask me,' said Mathews, the Commandant of the Alexandria Police Force, 'ask the Minister.'

'Are you saying the Minister authorized the search over your head?'

'I'm not saying anything; except that if you've got to ask somebody, then he's the one, not me.'

'You must have known. He wouldn't have instructed your men without going through you.'

'So one would have thought,' Mathews agreed.

'What the hell is this? Have you spoken to Henderson?'

Henderson was the Adviser to the Minister of the Interior.

'No,' said Mathews.

'I shall,' said Owen.

Mathews leaned forward and tapped his pipe out into a tray.

'Some things,' he said, 'have got a smell. When they have, it's best not to ask too many questions.'

'But, Christ, he can't do this over your head!'

'So one would have thought. But then, one goes on to think, he knows that as well as we do. So –'

'So?'

'He wouldn't have done it if he hadn't known he could do it.'

'That it was all right? That we would agree?'

'That's the way it strikes me,' said Mathews, 'after having been in the country a while.'

This was a jibe at Owen. Some of the old hands had not been pleased when a man had come in from India and been appointed to the senior post of Mamur Zapt.

Owen smiled.

'I'm surprised you're happy to let someone act over your head,' he said.

Mathews gave another tap to his pipe.

'I'm not happy,' he said. 'Just realistic.'

Alexandria, thought Owen, as he sat waiting for Mahmoud in a little café on the Rue de la Porte de Rosette, with its French place names, its *Bourse* and its *Place*, its neat municipal gardens and long promenades, was more of a French city than an Arab one. Or so he fancied. He had never actually seen a French city; hardly an English one, for that matter. He had been shipped out to India as not much more than a boy to join the Army there, and he looked now through Eastern eyes. Alexandria seemed to him a foreign city.

As, of course, it was, with its large populations of Greeks and Italians, the numerous businesses with foreign names, and, perhaps above all, the sign on the large building further up the street which spelled out reality in uncompromising terms: British Army of Occupation.

Part of its foreignness arose from it being the great international trading centre of Egypt. Here were the great international banks, here the stock exchange, and here the Appeal Court of the Tribunaux Mixtes, which dealt with cases, usually commercial, involving foreigners. And here, unsurprisingly, was the main office of the British Chamber of Commerce, which looked after British trading interests in the country, and whose chairman, significantly, had been one of the team accompanying the Governor of the National Bank to the meeting with the financiers in the Fayoum.

Looking now at the city through Eastern eyes, Owen suddenly saw how to some Egyptians, to a Mahmoud, for instance, that foreignness might seem oppressive.

'Minister?' said Mahmoud.

'Yes.'

Mahmoud put down his cup.

'That explains it,' he said.

'What?'

'What happened to me. First, I went to the local Parquet Office. They knew nothing about the search. So far as they knew, the investigation started when I arrived. So then I went to the police. They couldn't, or wouldn't, tell me anything.'

He looked at Owen.

'Now I know why. Well, after a while I realized I wasn't going to get anywhere. So then I asked about Strakhov. This worried them. Why did I want to know, they asked? I said I needed to know as part of my investigation. They went away and thought about it and then came back and said that Strakhov was nothing to do with the investigation. I said I was the best judge of that. Then they said I couldn't see him because he was being held under special provisions. Tell me about these provisions, I said.'

Mahmoud made a gesture of dismissal.

'Of course, they couldn't tell me. So then I said they were holding him illegally and demanded to see him. They were very uncomfortable but still refused. They would have to ask someone higher up, they said. Well, we went higher and higher and by the end of the afternoon we still hadn't got high enough –'

The copy of the will was waiting for them when they went back.

Mahmoud glanced at it.

'Made very recently,' he said.

'The week before he died,' said Demetriades. 'He came in one day and said he wanted to make his will.'

'On the spot,' said Atiyah. 'We had to do it while he waited.'

'He said that it was so that we would know what to do if anything happened to him.'

'If anything happened to him?'

'That's what he said.'

'Who are the beneficiaries?' asked Owen.

'There was only one; an old lady living in the Fayoum.'

5

When Owen got back to Cairo that evening he went straight from the railway station to an art gallery in the Ismailiya where he was meeting Zeinab. An exhibition was just coming to an end. Unusually, in that most cosmopolitan of quarters, it had been confined to native Egyptian art and, perhaps as a consequence, had made fewer sales than hoped. The proprietor, however, undaunted, had decided to hold an end-of-show party, to which Zeinab, who had friends among the artistic community, had been invited.

He saw her as soon as he went in. She was one of four women in the room – which was pretty advanced for Egypt, even in artistic circles – but the only Egyptian. Unmarried, there was no husband to put her straight on behaviour; nor was there much to be hoped for in that respect from her father, who was both a Pasha, and therefore did not care a toss for what anyone else thought, and a freethinker who liked independence in women, although not for the usual reasons; he thought it made them more sexually attractive. Zeinab had, therefore, been able to annex to herself a degree of freedom unusual in Egyptian women.

She was talking now, with some others, to the gallery's owner.

'All right,' he was saying, waving his arms excitedly, 'so it's traditional. It has to be if you want to make money. But one day, you wait, I'll put on an exhibition of exclusively contemporary Egyptian art!'

'You'll have a job,' said one of the people he was talking to, 'because there isn't any.'

'What about Abou?' objected someone.

'Abou is alive today: but that is his only claim to being contemporary.'

There were cries of protest.

'It is not that there is no contemporary art in Egypt,' said someone hotly, 'but that there are no critics who can appreciate it!'

'I quite like Abou's stuff,' said Owen.

'Hear the voice of the expert!' cried someone.

They all laughed. Owen's lack of knowledge of things artistic was a general joke in the circle.

Someone rushed, though, to his defence.

'It is because he is a Welshman. The genius of the Welsh people is for poetry not painting.'

'You've put your finger on it,' said Owen.

Someone took the fruit juice from his hand – Muslims all, they were drinking fruit juice – and replaced it with something stronger.

'What it is to be among friends!' said Owen gratefully.

He was used to their backbiting; but also to their warmth.

'It is good of you to come,' said the Golberg's owner. 'He's only just got back from foreign parts,' he told everyone.

'Alexandria,' said Owen.

'Isn't that a foreign part?'

'I must say it felt like it,' said Owen.

'All the same,' said someone, 'that's the place to be if you want to make money. All those Greek merchants wanting portraits of their children! Now, there's a chance for you, Yussuf!'

'I don't think I could.'

'Work for the rich?'

'Do portraits.'

'That is because he is such a traditionalist,' said the critic. 'Wasn't that what I was saying?'

There was no Muslim tradition of portraiture, not in Egypt, at any rate.

'I wouldn't feel comfortable.'

The artist almost shuddered.

'You see?'

'I don't feel comfortable even with that,' said the artist, pointing.

Further along the wall was a mummy portrait like the ones Owen had seen in the old lady's house in the Fayoum.

They all crowded round it.

'It is very good,' said someone, 'but why have you got it in your exhibition, Raoul? It is not art.'

'What is it, then?'

'An antique.'

'It is painting,' said the owner, 'and beautiful painting. What is that if it is not art?'

'It may be art,' objected someone else, 'but it's not Egyptian art. It's Greek art or Roman art. Not Egyptian.'

'Aren't mummies Egyptian?' asked someone. 'What is it to be Egyptian? Is it only to be Muslim Egyptian?'

Here, too, thought Owen, even in art, the questions of Nationalism arose.

He stooped to examine the portrait.

'Where did you get it?' he asked.

'Ah,' said the owner, laying his finger to his nose, 'that would be telling! And it's not for sale, either. It's only borrowed. A pity. Because if I could sell it I'd make a lot more money than I ever would from Yussuf's, or even Abou's, paintings.'

'That's the trouble,' said someone. 'In Egypt the excellence of the modern is always crushed by the greatness of the past.'

'In any case,' said Raoul, 'it couldn't be exported, you'd have to get a permit for it. It counts as an antique not a painting.'

'There you are!'

'There are people in Germany who would pay a fortune for this.'

'Change your line of business, Raoul,' someone advised. 'Go in for smuggling.'

'What a suggestion, with the Mamur Zapt here!' Then, in a mock whisper: 'Come back and talk to me later.'

They all laughed.

'Let's get an expert opinion,' said someone. 'What does our critic think?'

Owen examined the portrait.

'It's in encaustic on limewood,' he said, 'and could be from Hawara. The hairstyle and jewellery suggest a mid-Antonine date. There is an interesting mixture of Greek, Roman and Egyptian forms. The portrait bust is Roman, of course; the pose of the human figure is adapted from the Hellenistic Greek; but the context, I would suggest, is entirely Egyptian.'

Behind the veil he saw Zeinab's jaw drop.

'It must be another woman,' said Zeinab accusingly. 'You couldn't have thought that up by yourself.'

'I have to admit there was another woman.'

Zeinab pulled away from him sharply.

'It was purely platonic,' pleaded Owen.

'I'll bet!'

'Nothing physical took place between us. She showed me a few things –'

'Yes, I'm sure!'

'Which, all right, I did find myself responding to –'

'Yes, I expect you would have found that!'

'It's the kind of man I am: alive to the beauty of form –'

Zeinab sprang off the bed.

Cairo was where the Ministries were, so Cairo was where it would have to be unblocked. The next morning, Mahmoud went in to see his superiors about the obstruction he had encountered in Alexandria, confident that they would take up cudgels on his behalf. To his surprise, he found a distinct lack of interest.

'But this is important! It's a question of principle! Surely a Parquet officer should not be denied access –'

But the Parquet, which was usually very strong on principle, especially when it affected its own interests, did not seem anxious to take the matter up.

Mahmoud went higher, to the Ministry of which the Department of Prosecutions was part.

'There are important legal issues here. It touches on questions of rights –'

But the Ministry, ordinarily able to detect legal issues in even the most unpromising of subjects, could find none here. As for rights –

'But it is a question of principle!' said Mahmoud despairingly.

'Principle?' said the junior Minister doubtfully, as if Mahmoud was introducing some new legal term of dubious validity.

'Not to say the Ministry's standing!'

'We must judge issues on their merits, not in terms of their effects on the Ministry's standing,' reproved the Minister. He had not hitherto been noted for revolutionary pronouncements.

Mahmoud, stunned, withdrew to regroup.

He regrouped with Owen, pouring it all out to him as they sat drinking coffee at a table in the Ataba, the busy square at the top of the Mouski from which the trams and buses departed and where the clanging of the trams' bells, the whinnying of the buses' horses and the shouting of the vendors of peanuts, sugar cane, pastries and seditious newspapers drowned the confidences being poured out not just by Mahmoud but by, it appeared, at the tables round about, the rest of Cairo.

'I'll see what I can do,' said Owen. 'I'll have a word with Henderson.'

Henderson, the Adviser to the Minister of the Interior, was a small, sandy-haired Scot.

'Why?' he said uncompromisingly.

'It's to do with Tvardovsky's death. You remember Tvardovsky? He was the Russian who was –'

'I remember Tvardovsky.'

'Right, well. I'm helping the Parquet in an inquiry into the circumstances in which he died.'

'So?'

'Strakhov was a friend of his.'

'Aye, but what's that got to do with the case?'

'We think Strakhov might know something.'

'Like what?'

'Well, hell, until we've talked to him, how can we know?'

'Aye, but you must have something in your mind. This laddie of yours may have been friends with half the population but that doesn't mean they're all connected with the case. We must have something more to go on.'

'There could be a security issue.'

'Aye, well, yes, there could. But –'

'Tvardovsky had radical sympathies.'

'I see. And put his money where his heart was?'

'To some extent, apparently, yes.'

'Now, pardon me, was that in this country or in another?'

'He financed the seamen's home of which Strakhov was the manager.'

'Aye, I see the connection. But now, have you anything to link the home with what you might call an issue of security? In this country?'

'Well, no, that's what we want to talk to Strakhov –'

'Aye, but is it anything more than a wee wonder in your head?'

'Not at this stage, no, but –'

'Have you any charges which you wish to bring against Strakhov?'

'No.'

'You see, if there was, it could override. But as there's not, well, sorry, laddie, but we are unable to accede to your request.'

'But, Jesus, *you're* holding him on grounds of security!'

'Aye, but that's not security in this country. It's security in another country.'

Owen retired, fuming.

'But at least you've got something,' said Mahmoud. 'Another country? That sounds like extradition proceedings.'

He bustled off, terrier-like, to gnaw at this new bone.

As Owen was making his way through the tables, a voice hailed him.

'Captain Owen! What a pleasure! You are well, I hope?'

It was Mirza es-Rahel, the journalist he had encountered at the hotel in the Fayoum.

'And how are you getting on with your investigations?'

He made a gesture with his hand and Owen dropped into the seat opposite him.

'Slowly.'

The journalist laughed.

'Well, it is not surprising. In a thing like this you come up against interests at every turn. As, of course, Mr El Zaki has found in his efforts to get access to Strakhov.'

'You know about that?' said Owen, surprised.

'It is our business to know about such things.'

Owen wondered for a moment if it had been Mahmoud who had tipped him off but then decided it couldn't have been.

'You are well-informed,' he said.

'We intend to make a big thing of Strakhov, Captain Owen. It raises important issues.'

'It does?'

'The incarceration of an individual, even a foreign individual, incommunicado and without access to lawyers – it is not good enough. Captain Owen! Allow this to happen and what happens next? Are any of us safe? No. No, this raises questions that go deep and wide, and we shall see that they are asked!'

'Well, it's nice to see *Al-Liwa* making such a principled stand, Mr es-Rahel.'

The journalist looked slightly discomfited.

'Actually,' he said, 'why should I hide it from you, Captain Owen, when in this we are on the same side? We do have a particular interest as well. Mr Strakhov, at the time when he was so outrageously seized, was acting as an intermediary between us and Tvardovsky in a matter of very considerable importance.'

'You and Tvardovsky?'

'Yes. The fact is' – again the journalist looked slightly embarrassed – 'Tvardovsky had offered us financial support –'

'When you say "us" –?'

'The Nationalist Party.'

'The Nationalist Party? Tvardovsky offered the Nationalist Party financial support?'

'Do not sound so surprised, Captain Owen. We are a perfectly respectable political party. The government parties get offered support all the time!'

'Yes, but–' Owen shook his head. 'And you were prepared to take it?'

'Well, why not?' said the journalist defensively. 'We have need of money like any other party.'

'Yes, but from a foreign financier! The Nationalist Party above all? I am surprised at you, Mr es-Rahel!'

'It does sound odd, I agree,' the journalist admitted, 'and at first we were inclined to reject it out of hand. But when we talked to him we became convinced that he was sincere – sincere in his commitment to our ideals, I mean. And, in fact, it was not as bad as it sounds. Most of the money was given for a specific purpose. There was a project in the Fayoum that he wanted our support for –'

'Just a minute,' said Owen. 'Who was supporting whom?'

'He would give financial support; what he wanted from us was moral support.'

'Moral support!'

'Support at grass level. As a party, we have strong popular support, although it is in the interests of the British, Captain Owen, to deny that. What he wanted us to do

66

was mobilize the fellahin in that area behind the project. That was important because what he envisaged was a giant cooperative scheme to develop the Fayoum. There would be co-ownership of the land and all profits would either be ploughed back into the project or else distributed to members. And membership – a feature which particularly pleased us – would be confined to those who actually worked the land. What the scheme seemed to offer was a different approach from the one that the British are foisting upon us. You can see why we were so interested. And why the loss of Tvardovsky was such a blow to us.'

He looked at Owen.

'Tvardovsky *and* Strakhov. Both of them. It makes you think, Captain Owen. Or so I hope.'

'Crackpot!' said the Financial Adviser, as Owen stood beside him at the bar. 'Completely crackpot!' He put his glass down on the counter. 'Or else very clever. I told him it was crackpot when he came to see me that day beside the lake. "Look," I said, "you know these men. They're capitalists. They live on the return they make from their investments. Do you suppose for one moment that they're going to support a scheme like this? With nothing in it for them? In fact, with them being cut right out of it? It would be like turkeys voting for Christmas!"

'Well, he laughed then, and said: "They're not turkeys, Mr Allen, they're crocodiles!" "All right, then," I said, "so you've got to give them a bit of bait." He looked at me for a moment quite startled, and then he said, very seriously: "Maybe you're right, maybe you're right." And then he laughed and said: "Live bait. That's what they'll want, isn't it?" And I said: "I don't know about that, but I do know that if you put something like this to them they'll throw it straight out of the window."

'So he said: "What about the government, then? Would it throw it out of the window too?" "Look," I said, "it's not us here that you've got to worry about. Who knows what daft things we might agree to? Look at that Light Railway project that you're so interested in, who would have thought we'd have done something like that? It's not us you've got to worry about, it's the people back home. The House of Commons is full of Liberal free-traders at the moment and they'd think we'd gone mad if we put a thing like this to them. Cooperation? Co-ownership? Jesus, these blokes couldn't even cooperate to buy themselves a drink. Yes, thanks, I will have one.'

He took a large sip.

'Crackpot,' he said, 'completely crackpot!'

'But clever, I think you said?'

'Well, possibly. You never know with people like that lot at the lake. It doesn't pay to be too naive. They don't always show their hand. In fact, sometimes they show you something else. Deliberately. So that you won't spot what's going on.'

'And you think this scheme may have been something like that? A sort of blind?'

'I think it might.'

'The Nationalists seem to be taking it seriously.'

'Yes, well, they would.'

Along the bar Owen spotted Paul, his friend, the Consul-General's aide-de-camp, who was, in fact, the man he had come to the Sporting Club to see. He pushed his way through the crowd towards him.

'I don't see why not,' he said, when Owen had finished. 'It sound as if the Ministries are playing silly buggers. I'll have a word with the Old Man.'

The Khedivial Sporting Club, or the Gezira, as it was known, was on an island and to get to it from the city you had to cross an iron bridge and then go down a thick avenue of lebbek trees. It wasn't far but just far enough to make it advisable, in the heat, to take an arabeah, one of the horse-drawn native carriages. Owen had taken one to come over but now, as he came out of the club and looked along the rank, there was not one to be seen. He decided to walk back up the avenue and then look out for one when he got to the bridge.

Over to the north-west a circle of white palings marked the race track. There must be a meeting this afternoon for already the carriages were drawing up. Separated from the race course by a sandy road were the football, cricket and polo grounds. There must be a polo match on this afternoon, too, for grooms with strings of ponies were making their way in that direction.

The first part of his walk took him across the golf course. Some men were playing at the hole nearest him. There was a sudden flutter of wings and an outraged cry from the men and then one of the big, scavenging hawks of the city rose steeply, something white clutched in its claws.

'God damn it!' said one of the men. 'That's the second ball I've lost this week!'

However, such things were in the normal course of events on Egyptian golf courses. Another ball was produced and play resumed.

Out here in the open it was very hot and although it was only a couple of hundred yards, he was glad when he reached the shade of the lebbek trees.

There was a steady stream of people coming down the avenue towards him, some on horseback, some on bicycles and many, including whole families, in carriages. For Wednesday afternoon at the Gezira was one of Cairo's social occasions.

Among the riders were several men dressed for polo and usually with a groom beside them leading a string of ponies. One of them hailed him.

He looked up. It was Prince Fuad.

The Prince dismounted, gave his horse to the groom and then came across to him.

'Hello, Owen,' he said. 'Not staying for the match?'

'Not this afternoon,' mumbled Owen, almost guiltily. 'Work to do.'

'Ah, yes.'

The Prince fell in beside him and began to walk back up the avenue.

'Busy then,' he said. 'This Tvardovsky affair?'

'That and some other things, yes.'

'Damned nuisance,' said the Prince. 'I see that now. At the time, I thought: body, mess, must clear it up. Get it out of the way. That's the thing to do with bodies, isn't it? In this heat. Get them out of the way. When you're dead, you're dead. No use going on about it. Best get them underground. Trouble is, even when they're underground, they leave mess behind them, you've still got it to clear up. That's what you're doing, isn't it? Clearing it up.'

'Well, yes, I suppose so.'

'How are you getting on? Looking into background, that sort of thing? Going through his effects?'

'Someone else had done that.'

'They have?' Prince Fuad looked slightly dashed. 'Still,' he said, 'I daresay you'll chase them up.'

'I hope so.'

They walked a little way in silence. The Prince seemed to be deliberating.

'The thing is,' he said. 'The thing is, something of mine may be among his papers.'

'Really?'

'Some share certificates. Got my name on them. Belong to me. I was wondering – if you came across them, I'd like them back.'

'If they belong to you, then you can certainly have them back.'

'Got my name on them. That's the important thing. At least, that's what Tvardovsky said. "Your name's an asset," he said. "It's worth money." "Not enough," I said. "The bank's not willing to lend any more." "That's because you go about it in the wrong way," he said. "You tell me the right way, then," I said, "and I'll change overnight." "Just let me borrow your name for a bit," he said, "that's all."'

'He bought some shares in your name?'

'That's right.'

'What did he want to do that for?'

'Because he thought that at the last moment they might

70

restrict the offer to native Egyptians. That's what they'd done before, you see, with another company he was interested in. The Fayoum Light Railway. Well, I think he wanted to make sure this time. "You see," he said, "you're an Egyptian." "I am," I said, "and much good it's done me so far." "Things are about to change," he said. And then I shut up because I thought he was about to start again.'

'Start again! On what?'

'This damned project of his. Completely lunatic, if you ask me. The great Fayoum cooperative! I mean, I'm all for peasants working together, that's what peasants should do, but you've got to have someone telling them what to do or you'll never get anywhere. "You should see them on my estates," I said. "A bunch of idle sods! Always off in the shade. The only way you can get them to work is by putting a boot up their backside." "But that's because they're working for you," he said. "What if they were working for themselves?" "I don't want them to work for themselves," I said. "I want them to work for *me*!" He laughed and then said: "Well, Prince Fuad, I think it may be best if we restrict your contribution to lending us your name."'

'That was for this project in the Fayoum, was it?' said Owen, puzzled.

'No, no! I wouldn't have anything to do with that! It was completely lunatic, as I said. It wasn't just working together, it was, well, *everything* together! Complete equality. Well, I couldn't have that. "It's utter nonsense," I said. "You can't have a peasant equal to a Prince, or where will you be? It turns everything upside down." "Well, yes," he said. No, no, I wasn't going to have anything to do with that. I was only willing to let him borrow my name for the Covered Markets Scheme.'

'Covered Markets!'

'Yes. They had this scheme, you see, to build a covered market in every town in the Fayoum. So that it could take place in the shade. Well, I wasn't sure I was altogether in favour of it, in principle, I mean. After all, we've managed all

71

right without them up to now, haven't we? But they said, no, no, it will be better for everyone, better for the animals, the produce. "Look, Prince," said Tvardovsky, "it will be better for *you*, because we can make some money out of this." So I lent him my name.'

'And he bought shares with it?'

'Yes. In the Fayoum Covered Markets Company. But then he kept the share certificates. "It may be your name, Prince, but it's my money," he said. But now I'd like them back.'

'Ye-es. Of course, it was his money.'

'But my name. I mean, they're legally mine, aren't they?'

'I think we'd have to let the lawyers sort that out.'

'I don't think we need to bring the lawyers into this, do we? Surely not in the case of a Prince of the blood.'

'Well –'

They had reached the end of the avenue. Owen saw suddenly that the groom was riding behind them with the Prince's horse.

'A dammed nuisance,' said the Prince, 'him dying like that. He ought to have sorted things out first. He must have known.'

'Must he?'

The Prince glanced at him.

'Wasn't that why you had the gun?'

'Why must he have known?'

Fuad shrugged.

'People invest hopes,' he said. 'Both on the lunatic side and on the sane side. And then when they are disappointed –'

He snapped his fingers and the groom brought the horse up alongside him.

'He would have been all right if he had stuck to one side. The Covered Markets Scheme, for example. But when he started mixing them –' He shook his head. 'An egg,' he said, 'I've always said that he was like an egg. A rich Russian Fabergé egg. A fine piece of work.' He swung himself up into the saddle. 'But cracked,' he said.

6

'Truly,' pleaded Owen, 'she was about eighty.'

Zeinab, however, was still not entirely convinced, and, to make amends, he decided to buy her a picture. He returned to the gallery, where Raoul was in process of dismantling the exhibition. There were still some pictures on the walls, however, one of which, Owen remembered, Zeinab had particularly liked.

'Jesus!' he said, reeling back. 'That's two months' pay!'

'Cheap at the price!' urged Raoul.

'Yes, but –'

'I've got the artist to pay. And then there's my own costs: rent, publicity, that sort of thing. Not to mention advances here and deposits there. There's a lot of financing behind an exhibition, you know.'

'No, he doesn't,' said a voice behind them. 'My friend understands nothing whatsoever about finance. It is what holds him back in life.'

Owen turned. It was the woman he had met in the hotel in the Fayoum. 'Hello!' he said, surprised. 'What are you doing here?'

'Why shouldn't I be here?'

'I thought you had left the country. You know, that since you were with the Russians –'

'One of them, Boris, who lives in Alexandria.'

'There seem to be a lot of Russians living in Alexandria.'

'There are. It's a hell of a lot better than living in Russia. However, what I'm doing here is picking up a picture. That one,' she said, pointing to the mummy portrait.

'Natasha is returning it for me,' said Raoul. 'It was only borrowed.'

'Boris is interested in pictures?'

'Not to him. I'm taking it back to a friend of mine who lives in the Fayoum.'

'She wouldn't by any chance be an old lady?'

'Irena Kundasova? How do you know her?'

'Saw her only last week,' said Owen.

'Really?'

'How does she come to be a friend of yours?'

The woman shrugged.

'We Russians stick together. At least, out here we do.'

'Of course. She was a friend of Tvardovsky's, too, wasn't she?'

'A good friend.'

'You were a friend of his, too,' said Owen. 'You went to his tent that night.'

'I should have slept with him,' she said. 'Instead, we wasted our time arguing.'

'Over what?'

'I was trying to persuade him not to go out on a limb.'

'In case he was sawn off?'

She looked at him sombrely.

'There was always that possibility,' she said.

She turned to Raoul. 'How about that picture?'

'I'll wrap it up for you. It won't take a moment. You don't mind, do you?' he said to Owen. 'You could think about that picture.'

'I'm thinking about another one,' said Owen.

Raoul looked troubled.

'I'd like to sell it to you,' he said. 'But I've brought it down as low as I can already. Honestly! I've already given you a big discount –'

'Don't worry! I'll find another. It's just that I can't afford –'

'All right,' said Raoul. 'Another five per cent!'

'Hey!' said the woman. 'A double discount? You never do that for me!'

74

'He's a friend of mine.'

'Aren't I a friend too?'

'Sure. But he's the Mamur Zapt!'

The woman went still.

'Mamur Zapt?' she said.

Owen helped her carry the portrait out to her arabeah.

As it pulled away, he saw Zeinab standing beside him.

'About eighty?' she said.

Some hours of explaining later she consented to return with him to the gallery.

'I'll have that one,' she said.

Which wasn't the one he had chosen.

And more expensive.

'I'll let you have credit,' said Raoul sympathetically.

'For three months, please,' said Owen, resigned.

While Raoul was wrapping it up, and while Zeinab was looking at some pictures at the other end of the room, he said to Raoul:

'Who was that woman?'

'Natasha? She works for Savinkov. When I say works –'

'I know what you mean. Who's Savinkov?'

'A financier. Big. Interests everywhere.'

'What sort of interests?'

'Cotton? Doesn't he own cotton mills somewhere? With some Syrians? And wasn't there a big dust-up about some company he was interested in in the Fayoum? What was it, now? Something to do with transport. A Light Railway Company – the Fayoum Light Railway Company. Yes, that was it.'

In the Place al Ataba black-gowned, black-veiled women with baskets on their heads were hurrying to climb up into the unroofed, horse-drawn native buses, and dark-suited young office effendi with smart canes under their arms and red pot-like tarbooshes on *their* heads were jumping off the electric trams and rushing into the offices of Credit Lyonnais.

Everyone was hurrying, which was a pretty fruitless thing to try to do, thought Owen, given that the square was as usual blocked with arabeahs, carts, forage camels with their great loads of clover swinging down on either side, and sheep; not to mention loofah-sellers, lemonade-sellers looking like portable urns and hatpin-sellers looking like strayed hedgehogs with their pins sticking out all over them; not to mention sellers of every other description, standing casually in the middle of the road, to the fury of the tram drivers uselessly clanging their bells.

Mahmoud came through the tables towards him; not hurrying, just his usual brisk self.

'Yes,' he said, after the usual prolonged Arab greetings, which neither hurry nor briskness would allow to be curtailed, 'it is a case of extradition.'

'On what grounds?'

'Security, whatever that means in Russia.'

'It's Russia that's applied for extradition, is it?'

'Yes.'

'Well, at least we've got something.'

'Yes.' Mahmoud hesitated. 'Yes,' he said again.

'What's the matter?'

'It's still not quite right.' Mahmoud frowned. 'At least, I think it is not quite right. He appears to have been arrested merely on the Consul's oral request. Now that could be acceptable if there was a need for speed; if, say, there was a risk of the man fleeing, and there was no time to prepare a formal request. But then a formal request should quickly follow. So far no written request has been lodged, and it is now some weeks since Strakhov was taken into custody. I know what you are going to say,' he said hurriedly. 'You are going to say that sometimes administrative processes in Egypt are not as quick as they might be –'

He looked expectantly at Owen, who, however, certainly wasn't going to say anything of the sort.

'But even so! And, besides, a practice seems to have grown up in Alexandria of acceding to even merely oral requests of

Consuls. It is an informal – and illegitimate, in any view – extension of Capitulatory Privilege.'

Another questioning look; which Owen, again, carefully did not rise to.

'But that is not all. If that were all, then, perhaps, I would have to tolerate it.'

He grimaced. 'Tolerate! That I should say this!' said Mahmoud wryly. 'That anything to do with the Capitulations was to be tolerated, much less an illegitimate extension of them! But that – that is not the worst thing.'

He looked at Owen.

'He is being held incommunicado,' he said.

'Incommunicado?' said Owen. 'But –?'

'I know. It is not possible. That is what you will say. And yet he is. Merely on a Consul's word.'

'I'm sure –' began Owen.

Mahmoud held up a hand.

'He is not even being allowed access to lawyers.'

'Oh, come!' said Owen.

'I assure you!'

'I find this very hard to believe.'

'I find it hard to believe, too. But I have checked this very carefully. I have spoken to his friends and they tell me he has been denied permission to speak to a lawyer. I have asked the Ministry to give me details of his legal representation and they were unable to supply them.'

'But, surely, he can be extradited only after proceedings in court; and if there are proceedings in court, he must be legally represented.'

'One would have thought so, yes.'

'But –'

'You see now,' said Mahmoud, 'why I think things are, well, not quite right.'

'The Fayoum Agricultural Produce Company,' said Owen.

'Well, no, Effendi, I'm afraid not. We don't have the company details here. It's registered in London.'

'All right, then; the Fayoum Construction Company?'

'That's registered in Paris.'

'Fayoum Transport?'

'Moscow.'

'Meat Packaging?'

'London, again.'

'Bridges and Waterways?'

'Paris, I think. No, London.'

'Look, are all the companies in the Fayoum registered abroad?'

'Oh, no, Effendi. Just most of them.'

'What about Kfouri Cotton Mills?'

'That's a private company. We wouldn't hold the details here.'

'Where would you hold them?'

'Nowhere, actually. If it's private, it's, well, private.'

'Fayoum Sugar Cane?'

'That's a private company, too. In fact, it's the same private company. That is, it's another company belonging to the Kfouri Brothers.

'Who are the Kfouri Brothers?'

'Syrians.'

'It's not registered in Aleppo?'

'There's no need to. They're both private companies. What exactly were you looking for, Effendi?'

'I'm trying to track down the interests of a man named Savinkov.'

'I don't think you will find that here, Effendi. Mr Savinkov is a financier based in Alexandria.'

'I'm told he has interests in the Fayoum?'

'Very possibly. But you won't find them listed.'

'Why not?'

'I'm not sure that someone like Mr Savinkov works like that.'

'All right, forget Savinkov. Let's try Tvardovsky.'

Some time later:

'Look, I know he had interests in the Fayoum.'

'I think it's the same thing as with Mr Savinkov, Effendi: financiers like that often don't hold shares in their own names.'

'Then how the hell do you find out who owns what?'

'With difficulty, Effendi; as I am finding just at the moment.'

'Why are you finding that?'

'Have you heard of the Fayoum Light Railway Company, Effendi? It was floated a little while back. Unusually, subscription to its shares was restricted to native Egyptians. I have been set the task of finding out whether the restriction was observed. As you can guess, I am having difficulties.'

'The Fayoum Light Railway Company is one of the companies I'm interested in.'

'I'm not surprised, Effendi.' The Egyptian coughed a little, discreet cough. 'Effendi, I think you may find that some of your interests come together. It was widely rumoured at the time that both Mr Savinkov and Mr Tvardovsky were very interested in the Light Railway Company. But, of course, they are not native Egyptians. However, they were – or so it was rumoured – associates of the Kfouri Brothers. Who are native Egyptian. Or so they claim,' said the clerk, who was a Copt.

'The Light Railway Company is not a private company?'

'No.'

'And, presumably, in view of the restriction of ownership, it is registered in Egypt?'

'That is correct.'

'So the company's details are here? Could I have a look at them?'

'I am afraid not, Effendi. Somebody is working on them.'

'Could I borrow the file? Just for a short time?'

'I will go and ask him, Effendi.'

He went across the room to where a man was working behind a partition. A little later he came back.

'I am sorry, Effendi, he is unwilling to relinquish the file. He said he came in especially to consult it.'

'Oh, very well. Well, look, let's try another: Covered Markets.'

When a file was borrowed, a slip was placed in the space it had occupied. The clerk consulted the slip and then came back.

'I am afraid, Effendi, that he has borrowed that one, too.'

'God damn it!'

The clerk coughed his discreet cough.

'Do you read Arabic, Effendi?'

'I do.'

'Then perhaps, if you wished, you could consult my hand-written notes. As I told you, I have been working on the Light Railway ownership and have extracted many of its details. The names of shareholders certainly.'

'That would be very helpful!'

Unfortunately, it wasn't. There were the names, certainly, and some of them, he could guess, were front names for Savinkov and Tvardovsky: Mohammed Kfouri, for instance, and Osman Kfouri. And also, even, possibly Irena Kundasova Scitovsky – the old lady living in the house at Medinet, who, presumably, had lived long enough in Egypt to count as Egyptian for this purpose. But what were the hidden threads of meaning, what did it all add up to? It took a certain sort of person to read behind the record and Owen wasn't that sort. The clerk, no doubt, was. So was Owen's own official clerk, Nikos, another Copt. Copts were good at working the ways of bureaucracy. They'd had plenty of practice at it. Three thousand years. Yes, that's what he would do. He would get Nikos to come over here and go through the files. He'd like that.

He handed the notes back to the clerk and thanked him.

'Not at all,' said the clerk politely. 'It's not every day we get the Mamur Zapt here.'

The man behind the partition raised his head. As Owen picked up his tarboosh and prepared to go, he came out from behind the partition and went up to him.

'The Mamur Zapt? Tobin.' He shook hands. 'I work at the Russian Consulate. If I had known it was you, I would have let you have them. We could have worked alternately.' He glanced at his watch. 'Care for a coffee?'

There was a café along the road, in a little square where a large lebbek tree stretched out its limbs and provided shade. There was a dark, cool room underground but they chose to sit outside in the square.

'So,' said the man, looking at him curiously, 'we needed the same files.'

'It appears so.'

'Was that because we were looking for the same things?'

'Perhaps.'

The man laughed.

'Well,' he said, 'it's no secret. We're both interested in the Fayoum. That was the point of the conference, wasn't it? But I thought you would be giving us more of a free hand. Otherwise, why make it just for Russian financiers? Still, I suppose it's only reasonable to help some of the plums for yourself. That was a smart move the British worked over the Light Railway Company! It caught us off balance, I don't mind admitting. We'd never expected that – that you'd restrict the shares to native Egyptians only! Well, all right, no hard feelings. But you can't expect us to leave it at that.'

He looked at Owen.

'But then, you don't seem to be leaving it at that, either.'

'Well, no.'

It seemed to satisfy him.

'I suppose we couldn't expect that. All's fair, after all, in love and war. And business. So you'll not be surprised that we're trying again. Any more than we are surprised that you're using your advantage. We all have the benefit of being the Capitulatory Powers, but the British have the inside position!'

'Why are you interested in the Fayoum?'

'It was partly that fool Tvardovsky. He came to us and said that there was something there for Russia. If we could get Money interested. Well, we'd been trying to do that, get financiers interested in Egypt, I mean – after all, if you've got the privileges of being a Capitulatory Power, it's crazy not to use them – and we were getting them over for a conference anyway, and then Tvardovsky came along with this project of his –'

He shook his head.

'Of course, the project itself was of no interest to us whatsoever. I mean, a cooperative! Not only that, but one inspired by the ideas of Kropotkin. Kropotkin, for God's sake! An anarchist, a terrorist! Did he really think that the Tsar was going to encourage a Kropotkin-style cooperative? Or that financiers would put their money into such a thing? Crazy. Absolutely crazy.'

'Turkeys voting for Christmas,' put in Owen helpfully.

Tobin looked at him, startled.

'I'm not sure he envisaged poultry breeding as part of the scheme,' he said doubtfully.

'No, no. I meant it would be like voting for their own . . . the financiers, I mean . . . I mean, they'd favour free markets, wouldn't they?'

'Would they? I don't know. The men I've met have always favoured protected markets where they could keep everyone else out and make a lot of money. No, no, this was a quite different sort of economics, this was' – he lowered his voice – 'radical.'

'Radical?'

'Revolutionary, even. In Egypt, of all places. Where serious powers have serious interests. Oh, I know it was just another of his crazy ideas. But ideas are dangerous, Captain Owen, as we know only too well in Russia. They have consequences. And what consequences might an idea like that have in a country like Egypt? A workers' cooperative in a place where workers have never had a voice in thousands of years? Where there is an ordered society not very different, if I may say so, from my own, with a nobility and a revered monarch on top? And where, as I have said, serious powers have serious interests. No, no!'

The Russian almost shuddered.

'No, no, it cannot be allowed. Let such an idea gain currency and it soon becomes a weapon in everybody's hand. To think that we would go along with that sort of thing!'

'What did you go along with?'

'We agreed to let him come to the conference and put forward his ideas, knowing, of course, that they wouldn't get anywhere. But what we did take from him was that the Fayoum was somewhere with development potential. A place with prospects! Especially if handled in the right way.'

'And so you pushed the financiers towards it?'

'Exactly!' He smiled. 'Knowing that you British were doing the same. Cooperation! That is not how the world works, is it? Egypt is not a sweetie shop. It is a lake in which big crocodiles swim. That is something that Tvardovsky did not understand. Nor that swimming in a lake where there are big crocodiles is dangerous.'

Owen was just about to pick up the file of the following day's newspapers and retreat to the café to read them when his eye was caught by *Al-Liwa*. For several days now the newspaper had included an item on Strakhov and the items had gradually grown in prominence. Tomorrow's was well up on the second page spreading across part of two columns.

It was a common misconception, said the article, that *Al-Liwa* was against foreigners. It wasn't. It was just against the abuses inflicted on Egypt by foreign powers. It was opposed to them even when they were perpetrated on their own nationals.

Take the case of the unfortunate Russian incarcerated in the barracks at Moharren Bay. What had originally drawn *Al-Liwa*'s attention to this case was the suspicion – well-founded, it appeared – that Egyptian sovereignty was being grossly abused. That was bad enough; but through focusing one's attention on the larger issue it was easy to lose sight of an apparently lesser issue, the injustice being done to an individual. Foreign that individual might be, but while he was in Egypt he was entitled to the protection of Egypt's laws; and that protection was being denied him.

Mahmoud couldn't have done better himself, thought Owen, gathering up the newspapers. In the circumstances it was good that the issue was getting an airing, even if it was in a Nationalist paper. Well, this was one item that he certainly wouldn't be censoring!

The telephone rang. It was Paul.

'Gareth,' he said. 'The Old Man's a bit concerned about a story that *Al-Liwa*'s been running. Every day recently there's been a piece about a Russian down in Alexandria. Well, the Old Man feels it's not entirely helpful. Could you do something about it?'

'Paul, this is the man I spoke to you about. Remember?'

'Yes. And I *did* speak to the Old Man, as I said I would. And this is what he said: just at the moment, he would like you to hold back.'

'But why, Paul? Why does the Old Man want this?'

There was a long pause, as if Paul was deliberating. Then he said: 'I think it's because, just at the moment, he's got other fish to fry, big fish, and he doesn't want anything else in the pan. Sorry!'

Owen settled himself at his usual table and began to work systematically through the next day's newspaper, marking the passages he wanted deleted or altered. There were few of them, usually just those which he thought would inflame religious or ethnic tensions. Cairo, with its many different religious and ethnic groups and its multiplicity of nationalities was like a power-keg; one spark and the whole lot might blow up. Personal abuse and scurrilous stories, of which there were plenty, he usually left, on the principle that while sticks and stones might break bones, calling people names never hurt them; although this was not a point of view that everyone in the British Administration, nor any of the politicians, agreed with.

Of direct political intervention there was usually very little, partly because the Khedive's office had given up trying and partly because the Consul-General, or so Owen had assumed, couldn't be bothered. When there was, it was normally on the grounds that publishing the item would cause a riot; that is, on grounds of public order. Owen could not recall ever previously being asked to delete an item without a reason of this sort being given; and he felt very uneasy about it, so much so that he put *Al-Liwa* aside, leaving it till last. He hadn't quite got to it when he saw Mahmoud coming through the tables towards him.

He saw at once that he was out of sorts.

Over a cup of coffee he came out with it all to Owen. Armed with his fresh knowledge about the improprieties surrounding the application for Strakhov's extradition, he had gone confidently back to his superiors. The Parquet was normally strong on both matters affecting the individual and on procedure. To his astonishment they were as negative as they had been before. Annoyed, he had insisted on going higher, to the Ministry again, where, however, he had met the same response.

'I got nowhere,' he said. He was smouldering. 'They go on about the Capitulations all the time,' he said bitterly, 'and then when they get offered a chance to challenge them, what do they do? Back off!'

He looked angrily, but unseeingly, at Owen.

'All of them! Ministries, politicians – every one of them! "Give it a rest, Mahmoud!" they say. Give it a rest! There's too much giving things a rest in Egypt! Someone needs to get up and do something!'

He took a drink from his cup.

'It's like running into a brick wall,' he complained. 'Every-where, you get blocked. It's as if – as if they've fenced off an area and are allowing no one in. But why, I ask myself? Why can no one go in?'

He swallowed a great gulp of coffee, unaware that it was scalding hot.

'It is as if some decision has been made. This is a special

area and no one can go in. But why should that be? What is so special about it?'

He looked almost accusingly at Owen.

'What is so special about it?' he repeated.

Owen knew better than to reply.

'Shall I tell you what I am coming to think? I am coming to think it is because it is an area that someone, someone very powerful, has marked off on their own. Who could that be? There can be no doubt, can there? Not in Egypt. The only people powerful enough to do that are the Capitulatory Powers. This is something to do with Capitulatory Privilege. And not in a trivial sense; it is not just some foreign country abusing its power in a minor way, reaching out to seize a man because he has offended them. No, it is something much bigger. It must be bigger, for them to block like this. It must be bigger if –'

He paused.

'If,' he continued, looking at Owen, 'they are prepared to sacrifice two of their own people for it.'

'Russia?' said Owen.

Mahmoud laughed.

'I do not think of Russia as apart from the others. This is a group of foreign countries ganging up on Egypt!'

'Well –' said Owen.

'Including England,' said Mahmoud fiercely.

'Well –' said Owen again.

Mahmoud subsided.

'That is how I see it,' he said.

Owen shrugged. They sat there for some time in silence. Mahmoud's eye fell on *Al-Liwa*, now on top of the pile.

'It drives you back,' he said. 'It drives you back on the one group of people who are not blocking you.' He picked *Al-Liwa* up and opened it, then pointed to the article about Strakhov. 'You see,' he said, 'here, at least, we are not blocked.'

'Actually –' said Owen.

Mahmoud stared at him; not angry but puzzled. And then, as he stood up, not even puzzled, but sad.

*   *   *

When Owen got back to his office he found a confused, agitated message from the old lady in the Fayoum saying that the house in Medinet had been raided and wrecked. By the Tsar, she said.

7

The woman, Natasha, was waiting for them at the door.

'Yes,' she said, 'I told her to send for you. What is the point of having friends like the Mamur Zapt if you don't use them?'

'Where is Irena Kundasova?'

'Lying down. She is in a state of shock. She was wandering around when I got here, confused, disoriented. Eighty-five,' said the woman in cold fury. 'Eighty-five, and they do this to her!'

'Had she been physically attacked?' asked Mahmoud.

The woman looked at him, as if registering his presence for the first time.

'Mahmoud El Zaki,' said Owen. 'Parquet.'

Owen had, naturally, passed on the old lady's message and the two men had, as naturally, come together. Mahmoud, however, was distant this morning. On the journey up in the train neither had said much.

'No,' said the woman, 'but they shut her in a room. The servants heard her when they came the next morning.'

'It was at night, then?'

'She woke up early. She often does. She heard a noise and went to see. She thought perhaps a cat had got in.'

'She saw them?'

'Yes. There were two Arabs and a European. But I do not think she will be able to help you much. She is very confused. It all happened so quickly and in the dark.'

'But she did say there was a European with them?'

'Yes. But even that is not so simple.' She made a grimace. 'She thinks he was from the Third Section.'

'The Third Section?'

'It was a branch of the Tsar's Special Police. It dealt with suspected revolutionaries.'

'Well –'

'It was abolished,' the woman cut in. 'More than thirty years ago.'

'Oh!'

'It was the Third Section,' said the woman, 'who came for her husband. All those years ago when they were still living in Russia, before they came to Egypt. The shock – I think it carried her back, she is still very confused.'

'Let her sleep. Perhaps she will be more clear in her mind after. But a European, at any rate? That much is definite.'

They asked to see the rooms. The woman led the way in silence. She seemed to know the house well.

The sight was oddly familiar. Everywhere, cupboard doors were hanging open, the contents pulled out on to the floor. Drawers had been pulled out and simply tipped up. Anything closed had been opened. The valuable pots, the plates in their niches, had been left undisturbed.

The room most affected was the one that had been the old lady's working room or study. Here there were desks, two of them, one which was obviously hers and a bigger one which had probably belonged to her husband. The bigger one had a rolltop which had been forced. The drawers of the middle one had simply been pulled out. Letters were scattered everywhere.

The woman stooped and picked some of them up.

'These!' she said, shaking them in Owen's face. 'Her husband's letters to her! They read them. She had tied them with ribbon and they pulled the bundles apart. Her husband's letters! Her dead husband's! What good would they have been to them? Why do they do these things? Why?'

She burst into tears.

Owen tried to take her by the arm. She pulled away angrily.

'No!' she said fiercely. 'I will not cry. I will kill them!'

He managed to get her out of the room and took her to the takhtabosh, where he made her lie down.

He went back to the study. On his way he passed through the room with the wooden mastaba running along the wall and the mummy portraits opposite. Propped beside them, still in its paper wrapping, was the one Natasha had brought from the gallery.

In the study Mahmoud was standing beside the old woman's desk. He turned and showed Owen a handful of notes.

'They weren't looking for money,' he said.

They went in search of the servants and found them in the kitchen. As in many of the old Mameluke houses, the kitchen was an outhouse. Food had to be carried across the open courtyard to the dining room, but the disadvantage was outweighed by the comfort of having the heat and the smells kept separate from the part of the house used for living in.

There were four servants sitting shocked and silent on the stone floor. One was cook, one a gardener, one a houseboy, who cleaned the house, and one a youngster not much more than a child, who appeared to understudy everything. It was he who had raised the alarm. One of his duties was to light the fire in the kitchen before the others came, and as he was crossing the courtyard he had heard the old lady's cries. He had roused the others and they had gone together into the house and found Irena Kundasova locked in a storeroom. They had taken her to her room and tended her and then sent for the police.

'Was not the woman here?'

'The woman?'

'The other Sitt.'

Natasha had arrived later.

'But before the Mudir,' said the gardener tartly.

She had at once sent for the hakim, and he had prescribed

a pill for the old lady which had made her sleep for most of the rest of the day.

Meanwhile, Natasha had taken charge. They all knew her, she was often here, and had been content to leave things to her. She had spent the day by the old lady's bedside; except that when the Mudir had at last arrived, she had come down and chided him. She had refused to let him touch anything in the affected rooms.

'Leave that for those who know what they are doing,' she had said, much to the pleasure of the houseboy, who had then retailed this to the other servants and most of Medinet.

It was at this point that she had sent for the Mamur Zapt, taking the message along to the station herself. The mention of the Mamur Zapt had stilled the Mudir's protests and he had withdrawn to his office, leaving everything in the house as it was.

'That is, perhaps, as well,' said Mahmoud, 'although he should have notified the Parquet. But there were other things,' Mahmoud said wrathfully, 'that he should have looked to. The men came in the night. Has he checked to see if anyone saw them? They must have used a light.'

But the Mudir, it appeared, overwhelmed by the prospect of yet another encounter with the mighty, or, at least, the awkward, had made no such inquiries.

'The house,' said Mahmoud. 'Did he look to that? How did the men get in? Were not the doors barred?'

'They were, Effendi. I saw to it myself.'

'Then how did they get in?'

'There are windows above, Effendi.'

'Are not they kept barred, too?'

'Not always, Effendi. Sometimes the Sitt opens the shutters to let the air through.'

'And did she that night?'

The servants conferred.

'Effendi, I think so,' said the youngster hesitantly, 'for I saw that one of the windows facing on to the street was open.'

Mahmoud asked him to show him the window, and they all trooped round.

There were, as was usual with houses built in the style of the old Mameluke houses, no windows on the ground floor, the wall rising sheer to the box windows above. These were of the old meshrebiya sort, glassless and made of heavy, ornamented latticework. At one corner, however, there was a smaller window, put in later, still glassless but shuttered against the light.

'How could they have got up then?' said Mahmoud.

'A boy, Effendi,' said the gardener. 'They would have stood him on their shoulders and he would have been able to climb the rest. Then he would have gone down and unbarred the door.'

Mahmoud took the houseboy into the house.

'You know the house,' he said. 'Let us go through it together. And if you see anything that I do not see, tell me.'

They went through the rooms, the houseboy wincing at the sight, until they stood in the doorway of the old lady's working room.

'Tell me what you see.'

'Effendi,' said the houseboy, distressed, 'I see only confusion.'

'Go on looking.'

After a while, the houseboy said:

'Effendi, this is little, and perhaps it is not what you want, but the picture has been moved.'

'I am sorry?'

It was not, in fact, a picture but an ikon, standing above the old lady's desk, its two doors open like wings to show the head of a saint on the panel between them.

'It has been moved.'

'Moved?'

The houseboy went forward, took the doors in his hands and opened them out fully so that their backs were spread against the wall. The whole thing had been pulled roughly forward. The boy settled it back firmly.

'That is how it should be,' he said. 'That is all, Effendi,' he finished apologetically.

Outside in the corridor they heard the tap of a stick on the marble floor and a moment later Irena Kundasova came into the room, supported by Natasha. Her eyes went at once to the scatter on the floor.

'They do not change,' she said.

'You remember us, madame?' asked Owen.

She looked at him.

'You are the Mamur Zapt,' she said, 'and this nice man is from the Parquet. You wanted to know why Tvardovsky died. Well, have you found the answer?'

'There are more questions than answers.'

'That is true,' she said.

She hobbled across and looked down at the letters on the floor.

'They are from Nikolai,' she said. 'It does not seem right that they should be left lying on the floor.'

She went awkwardly down on her knees and began to gather them up.

Natasha dropped down beside her. The old lady gently pushed her away.

'No,' she said, 'this is for the widow. Your turn will come soon enough.'

'Mother,' said Mahmoud, speaking in the intimate voice of the Arabic, and not in the French that they had previously been using, 'they did not come for letters.'

The old lady sat back on her heels and looked up.

'No,' she agreed.

'What did they come for? Have you, perhaps, family jewels?'

'My necklaces!' said the old lady, struggling up in a panic.

The woman helped her.

'They are in my bedroom. They –' She stopped.

93

'But they did not come to my bedroom,' she said.

'Money?'

'What I have is in my desk.'

Mahmoud took the notes that were scattered around on the desk.

'Was there more?'

'I do not think so.'

'Valuables of any other sort?'

She raised her head.

'Our house is full of beautiful things,' she said proudly. 'It always has been. My mother –' She looked around confusedly. 'Our house is full of beautiful things,' she began again. 'Would you like to see –?'

Natasha led her gently back to her room.

'Effendis!' cried the Mudir, coming into the room with affected confidence. 'Have no fear! I will beat the truth out of them.'

'Them?'

'Ali and Mekhmet and Ja'afar.'

'You have seized the men who did this?'

'Not quite yet, Effendi. But I will!'

'Just a minute,' said Owen. 'How do you know it was Ali and Mekhmet and Ja'afar?'

'They are the thieves in this town, Effendi. It must be one of them. Oh, they will deny it and say they were with Bahija, or some slut or other. But I will get the truth out of them, never fear!'

Mahmoud showed him the money on the old lady's desk.

'Would Ali or Mekhmet or Ja'afar have left this?' he demanded angrily.

'They might have missed it,' muttered the Mudir, crestfallen.

'Or perhaps whoever did it was not Ali or Mekhmet or Ja'afar.'

The Mudir was silenced.

Briefly.

Then he started again.

'Effendi –'

'Yes?'

'Perhaps they were not looking for money.'

'Well, that is possible. Indeed, very likely.'

'But, Effendi, what sort of bad man is it who breaks into a house and, seeing money, does not take it?'

'Not the ordinary sort of bad man, certainly.'

The Mudir looked troubled.

'Effendi, I know all the bad men in Medinet –'

'They may well not have come from Medinet.'

'No? They came from somewhere else?' said the Mudir, brightening. 'Ah, well, there's not much I can do, is there? Not if they came from Abchaway or Abouxah. You'd have to speak to the people there –'

'Let us,' said Mahmoud, 'start, for the moment, somewhere closer. Medinet, for example. Check first if anyone has been seen looking suspiciously at the Sitt's house as if wondering how they might enter. Check next if anyone saw anything last night. Check, third, if there have been any strangers in Medinet. Ask at the railway station.'

'Effendi, I will! I will ask Tarik, he is always hanging about there. It is his job, you see, Effendi, he begs at the gate –'

Mahmoud began to go carefully through the rooms. After a while, Owen left him to it. This was a job Mahmoud could do far better than he could. The Parquet officers combined the role of investigating lawyer with that of investigating detective.

There was as well, ever since last night, a coolness between them. Mahmoud was unfailingly courteous but he had somehow put a distance between them.

Owen wandered out into the big central courtyard. The air was loud with the cooing of doves. They perched on the branches of a large sycamore fig tree which stood in the centre of the yard, its great branches offering shade to almost the whole of the yard, or waddled around in the dust, their rich feathers shining, almost sparkling, in the sun. The ones on the ground were mostly gathered in front of the takhtabosh, the long ground-floor gallery which ran the length of one side of the court and where they had first met the old lady. He saw now that they were picking at grain which had been thrown there, perhaps by Irena Kundasova herself.

Jasmine and roses hung round the columns of the takhtabosh and the mixture of scent, to someone like Owen with a keen sense of smell, was almost overwhelming. There was another scent mixed with them and it was only after a while that he realized where it came from. There were gates on one side of the courtyard which opened on to the river. On either side of the gates were tubs with orange trees in blossom.

He walked across to the gate and looked down at the water. A small boat was tied to the bank. It was full of onions and tomatoes, huge ones, the size of tennis balls and glowing with warmth and colour.

When you thought of Egypt in abstract you tended to think of desert; but it was equally valid to think of it as a garden. Where there was water as well as sun, things grew amazingly. And there was water in Egypt, where the Nile ran, especially, of course, but also in the Fayoum, where, over countless generations, man had extended the waters of the Nile so that a whole basin had become fertile and prolific.

Less fertile now, perhaps. The lake had shrunk. The soil had dried out and become desert. But might not the desert be reclaimed? That had been Tvardovsky's vision. Owen was no economist but, looking now at the giant vegetables in the boat, and almost intoxicated by the wreaths of jasmine and swathes of roses which hung everywhere, he was almost persuaded to share it.

Some men were coming through the courtyard. He recognized the cook and the gardener and the boy supporting them, but there was someone else with them, an old man.

They came up to the gate, greeting him shyly, and stood looking down into the boat. The old man jumped down and began to hand the vegetables up.

'Well, Abdullah,' said the cook, looking at the vegetables critically, 'these are fine tomatoes.'

'They are,' agreed the old man.

'It is the soil,' said the gardener. 'Over where you live, Abdullah, I think the land still keeps some of the wetness of the lake.'

'It does, but that doesn't mean it can do without watering.'

'Is all the land over there like that?'

'It is not just the water,' said the old man. 'Do you know what else I think it is?'

'No?'

'Shit.'

'Shit?'

'People have been shitting there for millions of years.'

'Yes, but they're not shitting there now, are they?'

'No. But this is where the great town was and I reckon they did lots of shitting in the past.'

'Well, I'm dammed! So this' – he picked up a particularly large onion – 'could have been grown on a Pharaoh's shit?'

'That's my theory,' said the old man.

The gardener took the onion and smelled it thoughtfully.

'It stands to reason,' he said, 'it could make a difference. If it was the Pharaoh's.'

'That's my theory, anyway.'

'Well, you are a fortunate man, Abdullah, to have the Pharaoh's privy on your land,' said the cook. 'That ought to be worth a bit.'

'It ought.' The old man looked worried. 'Perhaps I should have asked for more,' he said.

'More?'

'When I sold the land.'

'You've sold the land!'

'But, Abdullah,' said the gardener, distressed, 'why did you not tell me? I would have given you a good price for it. Especially in view of the privy.'

'Ah,' said the old man, 'but your good price would not

have been as good as the price I got. That was a big price from big men.'

'Big men?'

The old man laid a finger to his nose.

'And, besides, he was a friend of the Sitt.'

'What, not that daft effendi who was always poking around?'

'The same.'

'What the hell did he want your land for? I can't see him growing onions!'

'I don't know what he wanted it for and I didn't ask. Not once he'd mentioned the price he was willing to pay.'

'You really fooled him, Abdullah,' said the cook enviously.

'Fooled? It's good land. Although perhaps,' said the old man, winking, 'not quite as good as that!'

'Abdullah,' said the gardener, 'beware! When God smiles on you like this, you need to watch out. He's bound to have something else up His sleeve.'

The old man heaved the last string of onions up and climbed out.

'Well, perhaps He has. For now the Effendi has died.'

'What difference will that make now? For surely he has already paid you the money?'

'Only part of it. For I still work the land. "Go on working," he said, "for I have no need of the land just at the moment. And, besides, it is better if it is not known that I hold the papers. Let us not say too much about this. But here is some money now for your son's wedding and there is more to come. Meanwhile, reflect on what you want to do with it; for money is like dung – it needs to be put in the right place."'

'Well, that was wisely said. Only I would have asked for it all on the spot if I had been you.'

'I wish I had done. For now what happens, now that the man is dead? Who holds the papers? Who will pay me what is owed?'

'You would have done better to have sold it to me,' said

the gardener, 'for I would have given you cash. Especially if I had known about the privy.'

For a moment Owen thought it was a hyena entering the kitchen. He opened his mouth to shout. Then he saw that it was a man, horribly deformed and walking on all fours, so that his hip stuck up in a grotesque hump higher than his shoulders, giving his back the long tilt-down characteristic of the hyena. His head hung down. It was almost as if he was nosing the ground.

'Why!' exclaimed the gardener. 'It's Tarik!'

The Mudir came out of the house accompanied by Mahmoud.

'Greeting, Tarik,' said Mahmoud, dropping into a squat opposite him.

The man sat back on his haunches, almost like a dog, with his arms straight down to the ground before him.

'And to you, peace,' he replied, in a low, hoarse voice.

'The Mudir tells me that you sit at the station?'

'I do, Effendi. Every day and all day.'

'Then you see all who come?'

'I do, Effendi.' The man hesitated. 'Effendi, I know you seek for strangers. But yesterday no strangers came.'

'That surprises me, Tarik; for is not Medinet a busy station?'

'It is, Effendi, but it is busy with the ordinary people of the Fayoum coming and going; some to the fields or to the quarries, others to work on the roads or canals. Few come from Abchaway except those going to the hotel on the lake and none have come for the hotel this week. The only effendis who have come this week are Ferguson Effendi on Tuesday to inspect the Irrigation Works and a man yesterday going to the Kfouri Cotton Mills, and he is no stranger, for he has been here before.'

'The men we seek may not be effendis.'

'Still I would have seen them,' said Tarik positively, 'for I see all who come, and I know all who live in Medinet.'

'And there were no strangers among them?'

99

'None, Effendi.'

Natasha came downstairs shortly after.

'Irena Kundasova is asleep,' she said.

'Will she sleep long? There are questions we need to ask.'

'Probably not long. The old sleep in fits and snatches. But do not ask her any more, not just now. It is too disturbing for her. All this' – she gestured at the room – 'it has carried her back. She recognizes it.'

'Recognizes?'

'Once one has lived in a police state,' said Natasha, 'one recognizes such things.'

'Egypt is not a police state,' said Mahmoud.

'I thought so, too, when I came to Egypt, at first. But when I saw all this' – she looked around the room – 'I recognized it too.'

'This is not the work of the police,' said Owen.

'No? Well, that is what I said to myself. At first. Egypt is not Russia, I said. And so I sent for you. That was a mistake.'

'You should have sent for the Parquet,' said Mahmoud primly.

'No. Not that. That was not the mistake. It was only just now, when I was lying beside Irena Kundasova thinking how cruel men can be, that I realized.'

She turned to Owen.

'I shouldn't have taken so long, should I? Because you had told me that day by the lake when we first met. We made a joke of it, remember? You told me you worked for the Khedive, "in a general capacity," you said; and I said, in Russia we have people like that, too. And we both laughed. And then I forgot about it.

'But then, just now, lying beside Irena Kundasova, it came back to me. And with it, in my mind, a picture. It was of you. The morning that Tvardovsky died. You had just got into your boats, he into his, you into yours. You were right beside him. You had a gun, a different one from all the others, a small one. I saw it. I was watching from the bank. You took it out of your pocket and put it in another pocket. Where it could be got at more easily. And then the reeds closed behind you both and that was the last time I saw Tvardovsky alive.'

8

'You are quite mistaken,' said Owen.

Natasha shrugged.

'Am I? In my country when a man goes for a walk with the Head of the Secret Police and does not come back there is no need to ask what happened.'

'This is not your country, madame,' said Mahmoud.

'It is the same.'

'It is *not* the same,' said Mahmoud, stung.

'Why would I want to kill Tvardovsky?' said Owen.

'Because you are the Khedive's servant. Remember? You told me that day by the lake. At least you were honest.'

'The Khedive, then,' said Mahmoud: 'Why would he wish to see Tvardovsky killed?'

'Because he, too, is a servant. Their servant. He does what he is told. He has to. He is in debt and the British have an army here.'

'That has been true for a long time. Why should it suddenly be necessary to kill Tvardovsky?'

'Do you know what he said once? He said that the Big Powers were like crocodiles, waiting on the bank, ready to slide into the water when the moment came. Well, the moment had come.'

'Moment –?'

'That conference. It was going to be the first of several. They were going to take it in turns. To carve up Egypt. First, Russia, then the others. Another thing that Tvardovsky said: "It is when the crocodiles start cooperating that you really have to watch out!"'

She smiled, bitterly, to herself in recollection.

'Well, the crocodiles had started to cooperate.'

'What has all this got to do with Tvardovsky?' said Owen.

'He thought he could stop it. And he thought he might be able to do it then, at that very first conference. It was because they were Russians, you see. He thought they might listen to him. He said that, deep down, Russians understood these things. They do not naturally think in terms of competition. So he thought he might be able to persuade them – show them that there was a different way.'

'You mean that cooperative project of his? It never stood a chance!'

'Of course it didn't. You made sure of that,' said Natasha.

'You surely don't believe her?' said Owen, when she had gone.

'Of course not!' said Mahmoud.

He looked unhappy, however.

'But there are things,' he started to say, then stopped. 'This conference,' he began again. 'The secrecy. The obstruction!' He looked at Owen. 'And then the gun. Why didn't you tell me?'

'I thought it was obvious. I was guarding him. What else do you think I was doing there?'

'You had a handgun, yes?'

'Yes.'

'Which you took out of your pocket? And put in another one? As she said?'

'It got wet. It was in my hip pocket and the boat was full of water.'

'Yes,' said Mahmoud. 'I understand.' He hesitated. 'Why, precisely, were you guarding him?'

'I don't know.'

'You don't know?'

'They didn't tell me.'

'But, surely –?'

'The request came through in the ordinary way and I just

took it for granted that it was the usual – I mean, from time to time you get people coming through, and they say, stick a guard on him, and it's not because there's a specific reason, it's just that he's, sort of, generally important. Well, I thought this was another case like that. As I say, it came through in the ordinary way and the only thing special about it was that they wanted me, me personally, to do the guarding.'

'You personally?'

'Yes, I know it's a bit odd. I don't usually do anything like this myself, we have people –'

'But surely they must have said – I mean, when they said they wanted you personally –?'

'I assumed it was because they wanted someone who would blend in. Not be noticed. I mean, you wouldn't want it to be too obvious, these were important men, it was an important occasion –'

'How many other people were being guarded? Personally, I mean?'

'Well, none, so far as I know.'

'Just Tvardovsky?'

'Just Tvardovsky.'

'But –'

Mahmoud shook his head in incredulity.

'This was an important occasion. These were important men, as you said. And the only person being guarded was Tvardovsky?'

'It's not quite as bad as it sounds,' protested Owen. 'We did consider having a guard but decided not to. We thought it would draw attention. The Khedive wanted everything to be quiet. We thought that holding it out there by the lake would be enough. It's far enough from everywhere for us to be able to see people coming. They'd have to come through Medinet and we had people looking out there. The thing we were afraid of, you see, was an anti-foreign demonstration –'

'I see,' said Mahmoud drily.

'It doesn't look very efficient, I know –'

'No,' said Mahmoud.

He was silent for quite some time. Then he looked Owen hard in the face.

'My friend,' he said, 'have you told me all?'

'All!' said Owen, startled. 'Well, yes, I think –'

'You see,' said Mahmoud. 'It does sound extraordinarily inefficient. And I find that surprising, for to me the British have always seemed brutally efficient, at least, when their own interests are at stake. And so I wonder: is it so inefficient after all? That surely depends on what someone was trying to achieve.'

'I'm afraid I don't –'

'Well, no,' said Mahmoud. 'You wouldn't.' He laid his hand affectionately on Owen's arm. 'You wouldn't, my friend, because you are too generous. And too close. But you see, my friend, I ask myself why they asked for you especially as the guard and I think it was precisely because you are not, forgive me, an expert in this field.'

'To make it easy, you mean?'

Mahmoud nodded.

'That is one answer that one could give, yes.'

'Wouldn't it make it even easier,' said Owen, smarting, 'if they had said there was to be no guard at all?'

'Of course I have asked myself that; and the answer I came to is this: yes, best if no questions are asked at all, if the thing can be passed off as an accident. But if the questions do start being asked, what better answer could be given than, yes, of course the man was guarded. Indeed, by no other person than the Mamur Zapt himself! That,' said Mahmoud sympathetically but firmly, 'is what I am beginning to think, my friend.'

By now it was evening. There was a hotel in the town and they were about to set off for it when a message came from Irena Kundasova. She was expecting them for dinner, she said, and she herself would be coming down to join them.

'Of course one comes down to dinner,' she said, overruling Natasha's protests, 'when one has guests.'

It was a formal occasion, eaten round a large walnut table with glasses shining in the candlelight. There was sherry with the soup, wine for the main course and a sweet dessert wine to go with the fruit. Irena Kundasova merely sipped, Mahmoud, austere in this as in everything, took nothing and Natasha and Owen took the rest.

At one point the old lady looked around. She seemed puzzled.

'Where is Boris?' she asked.

'He has business,' said Natasha.

'Cannot he take time off even to eat?'

'He eats elsewhere.'

'You must look after him, my dear.'

'I'm hoping he'll look after me,' said Natasha.

The old lady laughed.

'Things are different from what they were in my day,' she said to Owen. 'Or perhaps they're not.'

After dinner she returned to her room and Natasha took them out to the takhtabosh, where they sat sipping their coffee among the fragrance of the orange trees.

'Mademoiselle,' said Mahmoud, putting down his cup, 'may I ask: who is Boris?'

'Savinkov,' said Owen, 'one of the Russian financiers.'

'You have been doing your research,' said Natasha. 'Of course, you would.'

'He was an associate of Tvardovsky.'

'That is right,' agreed Natasha. 'They worked together often.'

'Especially in the Fayoum.'

'That was towards the end. They had worked together in other places before. But the Fayoum was important, yes. It was why they quarrelled.'

'Why did they quarrel?'

'It was that crazy project of his.'

'The cooperative one?'

'Yes.'

'Savinkov didn't like it?'

'He didn't mind it being a cooperative. Boris is not like the others. He likes visions. He even likes Kropotkin, up to a point. That was why he and Tvardovsky got on together.'

'What didn't he like about it, then?'

'The wrong place. The wrong time. It cut across other projects, when they were far advanced. He tried to persuade him to drop it. He kept on trying. He was still trying even at that hotel by the lake.'

'Did he send you to try?' asked Owen.

'That night? No, that was my own idea. We had made love and afterwards I couldn't sleep. I got up and went outside. I saw the light in Tvardovsky's tent and I thought, well, that perhaps he might listen to me.'

'And did he?'

'When Tvardovsky believed in something, he believed in it absolutely. He was all afire. One idea sparked off another. It all came out in one great cascade. Listen to me?' She laughed. 'When he was in the grip of one of his big ideas he wouldn't listen to anybody. It took him over completely, there was no stopping him.'

She caught herself.

'Except,' she said bitterly, 'that someone did stop him.'

Owen and Mahmoud decided that it was too late now to go to the hotel and that they would sleep outside in the courtyard. The servants brought them bed-rolls and they took them out beneath the sycamore, where the moon would not shine in their eyes. Neither of them said anything as they unrolled the mattresses.

In the morning Mahmoud was nowhere to be seen. When Owen inquired of the servants, they told him that he had got up early and caught the first train.

'To Cairo?' said Owen, surprised and a little disconcerted.

'To Abchaway.'

He would, it appeared, be back later. Owen, after some

thought, decided to wait for him. Meanwhile, he went for a walk in the town.

The market was in full swing. Chickens ran about among the stalls. While they could. Every so often a hand descended on them and lifted them up. Then they were either thrust living into baskets or had their necks wrung. On the stalls themselves the vegetables glowed in the sunlight. The redness of the tomatoes seemed to burst out from them and hang in the air. The blackness of the eggplants took on rich, astonishing tones.

Everything was huge. The grapefruit were as large as footballs, the melons so ridiculously heavy that one was all a man could lift. Even the fish, hanging head down from a bar above the stall, were gigantic. Used as he was to Egyptian markets, Owen was surprised by this one; testimony to the bountifulness of the Fayoum, he supposed.

Even while he watched, however, the sun, which had been bestowing such richness, began to take its toll. Some of the stalls were in the shade of the trees. On those that were not, the produce began to wilt. Lettuces lost their freshness, beans their fatness. The oranges and lemons and apricots suddenly began to look dried up, the tomatoes and eggplants to look pinched.

'The sooner you get into the new covered markets, the better!' he said to one of the stallholders.

'You're right there!' said the stallholder, wiping the sweat from his face with the sleeve of his galabeah. 'I can't wait!'

'Well, I can,' said the man on the stall next to his, looking up. 'At the moment we can put our stalls here for nothing. In those new covered markets they're going to charge you.'

'It'll be worth it, though.'

'Yes; for the people running the markets!'

'You say that, Ibrahim, but I bet that when the markets go up, you'll be one of the first people in!'

'I'll have to be, won't I? Because that's where the people will be. But I tell you this: it's not the likes of you and me who are going to benefit from this. We're not going to be any richer. The only people who'll make money out of this will be the Kfouri Brothers.'

'Kfouri Brothers?' said Owen. 'Aren't they the people who own the cotton mills?'

'And about everything else in the Fayoum as well,' said the stallholder sourly.

'I remember them when they were just shopkeepers,' said the first stallholder. 'Now it seems they can buy anything. I don't know where they get the money from.'

'And they're the ones behind this Covered Markets Scheme?'

'So they say. Which means that the likes of you and me, Ibrahim, can't expect many favours.'

'That's just what I was saying, Abdul. We'd be better off as we are.'

The first stallholder looked along the row of stalls. All those in the sun were deserted. What people there were – it was getting late in the morning – were congregated about the ones in the shade.

'I don't know about that, Ibrahim. They say that the new markets will be wonders of the world! Even the ones for sheep and cows will have roofs on them. And running water, too.'

'Running water? For animals!' said the second stallholder, scandalized. 'I tell you, you're better off being a cow than a person in Egypt nowadays!'

Back in the house, Owen found no one about. The servants were in the kitchen, the old lady and Natasha presumably upstairs. Although the shutters had remained closed, the temperature in the house had crept up and in all the lower rooms it was unpleasantly hot. With the exception of the dining room, which had been cleared for the meal the previous evening, the rooms were exactly as they were when he and Mahmoud had arrived. Owen wondered when Mahmoud would allow them to be tidied. When he returned, presumably.

There was a footstep in the corridor outside and Irena

Kundasova appeared in the doorway. She came into the room.

'Why!' she said. 'What a mess! Someone must tidy it up.' She looked across the room. 'The ikon!' she said. 'It has been put back. How thoughtful of someone! Was it Abdul?'

She went up to it and patted it fondly.

'Irena Kundasova,' said Owen, 'why did they move the ikon?'

She looked at him in surprise.

'To look behind it. That's where people often keep their letters in Russia. That's where they always look,' she said.

Along the corridor he heard voices. A burly man of about fifty, dressed in an immaculate white suit, came into the room.

'Boris!' said the old lady with pleasure.

The man bent over and kissed her hand.

'Irena!' he said, retaining her hand and caressing it gently.

'Where were you last night? You should have been here.'

'I know. I had to see someone and they made me stay.'

'You will make Natasha jealous if you carry on like that.'

'I know. It was a mistake.'

She touched his cheek and left the room. A little later Owen heard her talking to Natasha at the other end of the corridor.

The man turned to Owen and came across, hand outstretched.

'Savinkov.'

'Owen.'

'Oh, yes. The Mamur Zapt. Natasha told me she had sent for you. It was kind of you to come. But – to come for this? A petty burglary?'

'Perhaps it was not petty.'

'Not petty?' The Russian seemed puzzled.

Owen said nothing.

'Forgive me,' said Savinkov hastily. 'I have no wish to interfere. But Irena Kundasova is an old friend of mine and I am concerned for her. A thing like this is a shock to someone of her age. I came at once to see if I could lend her any assistance. The Russian community in Egypt is a small one and we are very close. So when Natasha said she needed help – But, Captain Owen, if this is *not* a petty burglary, then she needs help even more!'

He looked round the room.

'But what makes you say that this is not a petty bur-glary?'

Owen pointed to the notes still lying on the top of the desk.

'Petty thieves don't usually leave the money,' he said.

'Well, no, but – something other than money, perhaps?'

'What would that be?'

'Valuables of some sort? There are many beautiful things in the house.'

'None of which appear to have been taken.'

'I see. Yes, well, that is puzzling, I admit. But, Captain Owen, excuse my saying so, is that enough to bring the Mamur Zapt here? The Parquet, yes, I can understand that. But the Mamur Zapt?'

'Irena Kundasova and I had met before.'

'Yes, yes, I have heard about that . . . That was to do with Tvardovsky, was it not?' He hesitated, and then seemed to make up his mind. 'Captain Owen – please, I am not asking this out of idle curiosity – could this break-in also, by any chance, be something to do with Tvardovsky?'

'Possibly.'

'I ask as a friend of his, a close friend, perhaps his closest. It was I who looked after his body.'

'You looked after his body?' said Owen, surprised.

'Well, yes,' said Savinkov, surprised in his turn. 'I was there, if you remember. At the hotel.'

'I thought it was the Consul who looked after the body?'

'The formalities, yes. But when a friend dies there is more to death than formalities. I stayed with the body. I wished to – I wished . . . I suppose, to give him company. Natasha, also.'

111

'You were the one who saw that the body was cremated? Why was it done so quickly?'

'Well, Captain Owen, you must know that. It was the heat – in this country you have to –'

'Yes, yes, I know. But there were things that should have been done first, examinations that ought to have been made.'

'The Consulate was supposed to be looking after that side. If things were not done exactly as they should have been, then I am sorry, but –'

His voice died away.

'Captain Owen, am I to suppose, from what you say, that those examinations were important? That there was something that made them, perhaps, especially important this time?'

'You may suppose that.'

'Captain Owen – please! – what was that?'

'Doubt about the circumstances in which he died.'

'Ah!'

Savinkov sat down suddenly.

'It was, then, as Natasha said?'

'It was *not* as Natasha said,' corrected Owen firmly. 'If what she said was the same as what she said last night.'

Savinkov waved a hand apologetically.

'I know, I know. She told me. Please forgive her. She thinks that all countries are like Russia, all police forces are like the Okhrana. But that is not important. What is important is that she said – she said that Tvardovsky's death was not an accident. Is that so?'

'There are doubts.'

'Captain Owen, you were there and I was there. I certainly thought it was an accident. Are you telling me now that it wasn't?'

'Mr Savinkov,' said Owen. 'You asked me earlier if this break-in was anything to do with Tvardovsky. The answer is: possibly. And the reason why we think that is that it resembles a break-in that was made into Tvardovsky's property after his death. In that case certainly and in this case probably the break-in was carried out by people who were not ordinary thieves. In neither case were they searching for money. I wonder if you, as a friend of Tvardovsky, have any idea of what they were searching for?'

Savinkov seemed taken aback.

'I? No, I'm afraid —'

He seemed, however, to be thinking: thinking, it appeared to Owen, more than ordinarily deeply.

Late in the afternoon Mahmoud returned. He made straight for Owen.

'I have been over to the hotel,' he said. 'I wanted to speak to your boatman.'

'Well?'

'It was as you said.'

He laid his hand apologetically on Owen's arm.

'I had to make sure,' he said.

Mahmoud spent the rest of the day working through the wreckage left by the break-in, at the end of which he gave permission for everything to be tidied away. The next morning he and Owen returned to Cairo and Owen went into his office to catch up on what had been happening in his absence.

Not a lot, it appeared; except, said Nikos, that a Mr es-Rahel had rung repeatedly. Owen guessed that it would have been to protest about the censorship. He glanced through the latest number of *Al-Liwa*. There was no mention of Strakhov. The censorship, for good or ill, appeared to be holding. He saw no reason to return the calls.

Just as he was leaving the office, es-Rahel rang again. It was not about the censorship. It was to say that Strakhov was being deported: the next morning.

'Deported?' said Owen, stunned. 'But he can't be! There have been no proceedings.'

'There aren't going to be any. He is being deported by direct order of the Minister.'

113

'But –'

'He would have gone already had it not been for us. He managed to smuggle a message out and we were able to secure a delay. But only for twenty-four hours. He will be deported tomorrow; unless, Captain Owen, you can do something to prevent it.'

9

'I'm just on my way to the opera.'

'I know, Paul, but –'

'And the Old Man's off to play bridge.'

'Look, Paul –'

'And what are you doing at the office, anyway? That's a strange place to be at this time in the evening. Have you no sense of priorities?'

'Paul –'

'Interrupt the Old Man when he's doing something important? No, I don't think I could do that. And would it be a good idea, anyway? Suppose he'd just lost a ruler or a rubber, or whatever strange thing he always seems to be losing when he plays cards? What would he say? I think he would say: "Someone's got to suffer for this, and it might as well be a Russian." I think that's what he'd say, so where would it get you? No, Gareth, I really don't think, in all conscience, that I could approach the Old Man.'

'Paul, *please* –'

'No, no, altogether a bad idea.'

'Paul –'

'I don't think it would be fair to bother him. As a matter of fact, I don't think it's fair to bother superiors at all. Much better to do it yourself.'

'What!'

'I'll just send a telegram – I could do that on my way to the opera – saying that instructions have come from the Admiralty that Strakhov is to be held for a further forty-eight hours.'

'The *Admiralty*?'

'Yes, it will puzzle them, too. Not to mention the Admiralty, when they inquire there. And by the time they've sorted it out, the forty-eight hours will have elapsed.'

'You don't think, Paul, that, well, questions might be asked?'

'If they are, I shall say that they've completely misunderstood a casual inquiry from a travelling Russian bootblack salesman.'

After he had put the phone down, Owen sat for some minutes thinking in the increasing darkness of his office. Then he rang the offices of *Al-Liwa*, which, like most newspapers, worked late.

'Mr es-Rahel? Owen here. I think we have forty-eight hours' grace. Now, naturally, we shall be doing all we can; but it did occur to me that a well-placed article in your newspaper could be of help. Yes, it is a reversal of policy, you could say that. But circumstances change, don't they, Mr es-Rahel, and we have to change with them. Flexibility is the watchword of the government this week, so I think an article on the subject might well creep through. There's still time to catch tomorrow's edition – no, there's no need to show it to me beforehand. On this, as on all things, Mr es-Rahel, I'm sure I can trust you –'

After he had finished going through the next day's newspapers, Owen gathered them up into a bundle and took them into Nikos's office and dropped them on his desk. Nikos, too, worked late; in fact, Owen was not sure that he went home at all.

'Any of them you want anything done about particularly?' asked Nikos, continuing to concentrate on his neat rows of figures.

'All of them.'

'All of them?' Nikos swivelled round in astonishment.

'Yes. A surprising omission, which I'd like you to point out to them.'

'We don't usually point out omissions,' said Nikos doubt-fully.

'We will on this occasion. It's an interesting story that *Al-Liwa* has got hold of.'

'*Al-Liwa*?' said Nikos incredulously.

'Yes. It is to do with a Russian named Strakhov.'

'There's nothing about a Russian named Strakhov in tomor-row's *Al-Liwa*,' said Nikos, who read all the newspapers beforehand too.

'There will be. They can get the details from Mirza es-Rahel.'

'Mirza es-Rahel?' said Nikos, reeling.

The next morning, early, Owen went to the Abdin Palace and called in at the Khedive's office, where he found the man who had liaised with him over the arrangements for the conference in the Fayoum.

'Why was a guard placed on Tvardovsky? Because someone asked for it, I suppose,' said the man indifferently.

'Who?'

'You really want to know? After all this time?'

'Yes.'

The man from the Khedive's office sighed. It was clearly going to be that kind of a day. He rang the little handbell on his desk and a lackey came in.

'The financiers' conference in the Fayoum: bring me the papers.'

He turned back to Owen.

'It would have been someone awkward. The Russians, I expect, since it was mostly Russians who were there. But why bother? What, after all, is a financier between friends? Or between enemies, for that matter. We weren't even putting a guard on His Highness. We discussed that, didn't we? Only we felt that in a place as remote as that, there was no need. I remember Prince Fuad being particularly firm on that point. "A threat," he said, "could come only from the Nationalists; and since they're all half-educated city-dwellers, they'd never be able to find their way to a place like that." In fact, he was rather doubtful if we could, either. The only thing that persuaded him in favour of the place was the possibilities for shooting.'

'Yes, yes,' said Owen patiently.

'And, really, it wasn't such a bad idea. The Russians took it up at once. We wanted to arrange something special, you see; and what do foreigners think of when they think of Africa? "Game," said Prince Fuad, and of course, he was quite right. I know Egypt hardly counts as Africa – Egyptians shudder at the thought – but for foreigners it does. And I know that nowadays there's no big game in Egypt – and I have no intention of going to the provinces to find out, it's mostly snakes and scorpions, as far as I can tell – but Prince Fuad said that ducks would be all right. "It's still shooting," he said, "and that's the main thing. It will make them feel that they're big boys; and then they'll give me lots of money." Which it looks as if they may do. So, on the whole,' said the official, 'it worked out rather well.'

'Except for Tvardovsky.'

'Tvardovsky? Oh, yes.'

The lackey came in with a bulging file. He put it on the official's desk.

'Well, open it,' said the official impatiently.

The lackey opened it and the official began to riffle through the papers.

'Actually,' he said, after a moment, 'it looks as if it wasn't the Russians after all.'

'Who did ask for the guard, then?'

The official picked up a piece of paper and looked at it, surprised.

'It rather looks as if Tvardovsky asked for the guard himself,' he said.

'You are spending,' said Zeinab accusingly, 'rather a lot of time in the Fayoum.'

'Well, yes, unfortunately. The old lady I mentioned –'

'The young woman I saw?'

'There are two of them. An old lady *and* a young lady.'

'And they both happen to live in the Fayoum?'

'The old lady does. The young one was just visiting.'

'At the same time as you?'

'The old lady's house was broken into. The young one happened to be there – she was returning a picture – and sent for me.'

'She didn't send for the police or the Parquet or the Mudir? She sent for you, personally? Since when have your services been available on a personal basis? Official services, I mean.'

'She knew I had been there before.'

'Well, yes, you're always there.'

'Asking about Tvardovsky.'

'So she sent for you? Seeing at once that a break-in was a political matter?'

'As it happens, it could well be a political matter. In so far, at least, as it connects with Tvardovsky. Mahmoud thinks so.'

'Ah, Mahmoud!'

'We're working on this together.'

'He covers up for you, and you –?'

'There's nothing to cover up for, for Mahmoud.'

'But there is for you? Well, yes –'

'*Neither* of us are covering up for anything. We've got nothing to cover up. We're just working on a case, that's all. And, as a matter of fact, about our biggest problem is that everyone *else* is covering up.'

'Oh, everyone else? That is a good story. That is a clever twist. You wouldn't have thought it up for yourself. Did she think it up for you? As she thought up all that stuff about the mummy portrait?'

'That bloody mummy portrait!'

'As a matter of fact,' said Zeinab sullenly, 'I have a message for you. From Raoul. About a bloody mummy portrait.'

He managed to persuade Zeinab to go with him. As they sat

in the arabeah, driving along the Imad ed Din, an idea came to him.

'Look,' he said, 'why don't we go away together for a week-end? I have been spending a lot of time out of town recently, I admit. Why don't we take a break? Just the two of us?'

'Well –'

'We could go to the Fayoum,' he said, with sudden inspiration. 'That hotel!'

'That woman!'

'No, no. She'll be miles away. She lives somewhere else. Alexandria, I think. Why not? Get away from Cairo, the heat, the smell, the dust –'

'But get away to what?'

'The hotel! It's a lovely situation – water, trees, everything green. We could go for walks by the lake –'

'What would we do?' said Zeinab.

'Well, as I say, go for walks. Look at things,' said Owen, losing confidence.

'Like what?'

'Well – birds.'

'Birds!'

'Pelicans, flamingoes –'

'Well, that's nice,' said Zeinab. 'Is there any music? Apart from the birds, I mean? Theatre? Art galleries?'

'We could go to Medinet,' said Owen. 'There are lovely old wooden bridges, water-wheels, beautiful houses with terraces, balconies –'

He sold it to her on the strength that it was Venice.

'It is about a man in Alexandria,' said Raoul. 'He is dead. Now, among his effects there is a really beautiful mummy portrait, and I just wondered if somehow you –'

'Tvardovsky? Was that his name?'

'Well, yes,' said Raoul, staring. 'You know him?'

'Do I know him! Yes, and I know the portrait.'

'Then –?'

'It's all in the hands of the lawyers –'

120

'Their names?' said Raoul, reaching for a pencil.

'Demetriades and Atiyah. But he left a will. The portrait will be covered by that.'

'You have no idea of the principal beneficiaries?'

'He left everything to an old lady, living in the Fayoum. You probably know her. She's the one who lent you that mummy portrait you had the other day in your exhibition –'

'Irena Kundasova? Well, I don't know her but Natasha does. I'll get her to speak to her. Although,' said Raoul, his face falling. 'I know she likes to hold on to her pictures. Still, Natasha – funny about that – the picture going to Irena Kundasova. But not so strange, I suppose. These emigrés all hang together. It's a pity he didn't leave it to someone else, though, someone less interested in art. Still,' he said, brightening, 'perhaps she'll feel she's got enough of that sort of thing already. At her age. Yes, that's what I'll do,' he said enthusiastically. 'I'll get Natasha to speak to her. By the way, have you seen Natasha's latest? No?'

He led the way to where some watercolours were hanging.

'This one!'

It was a view of Medinet: old houses framing an arched bridge.

'Nice, isn't it? At the amateur level. She's done several. She liked Medinet. She says it reminds her of Venice.'

'Venice!' said Zeinab, looking at Owen.

'What is it this time, then?' said the Financial Secretary, making room for Owen at the bar. 'Want some advice about how to handle your pocket money? My turn, I think. Whisky-soda, isn't it? *Wahid whisky-soda*!' he called. 'No, make that two. *Etnein*!'

'Cheers! No, not this time. I want to know about the Fayoum.'

'Is the Khedive thinking of holding another conference there? Good idea! Lovely spot. Only tell him to make it a bit longer this time so that I can get some fishing in.'

'Not as far as I know. But I just may not know. There's a story making the rounds that the conference was intended to be the first of a series.'

'Oh, yes,' said the Financial Secretary noncommittally.

'Why would that be? What's so special about the Fayoum?'

'Nothing's special about the Fayoum, except that, as you've seen, it's a fertile place. If you want to grow anything, that's the place to do it. And, just at the moment, with the international cotton price so low, we're wondering what else Egypt could grow. There's plainly a need for diversification.'

'Fruit, vegetables, that sort of thing?'

'Don't forget grass. Grass grows there, too, and where you have grass you can have cows and sheep. Still, other countries can probably grow cows better. No, the most likely possibility is grain.'

'The Fayoum was once the granary of Rome. Or so Tvardovsky said.'

'Tvardovsky, of course, was on to this early. Financiers tend to work these things out ahead of the rest of us. Mind you, not that far ahead. The government's been thinking about the development of the Fayoum for some time.'

'According to Tvardovsky, the key was water.'

'The trouble with water is that you can't think of the Fayoum in isolation from the rest of the country. Take water off higher up and you leave less for those lower down, like the farmers of the Delta. That's why we've been concentrating so far on building an infrastructure: a really good light railway system, roads, bridges, even schools.'

'And for that, of course, you need money. That was the other thing the Fayoum needed, Tvardovsky said: money.'

'Well, yes.'

'Was that what that conference was about?'

'Actually, no. They would have liked it to have been about that. But we are holding them off. We don't want everything in the Fayoum to be in the hands of foreign investors. We've even gone so far, in the case of the light railways, as to confine the holding of shares in the company

122

to native Egyptians. And we may well do the same in other cases, too.'

'The covered markets?'

'Possibly. The trouble is,' said the Financial Secretary, swishing the ice round in the bottom of his glass, 'that however much we try to keep the foreign capitalists out, the buggers will keep sneaking in!'

Further along the bar Owen saw the Chairman of the British Chamber of Commerce, up for the day from Alexandria to plead, no doubt, some unlikely commercial cause, and wormed his way through the crowd towards him.

'Of course I know about the policy!' he said huffily. 'Keep foreigners out! And a good thing, too. But do you know what? You'll hardly believe this. The damned fools have classed British as foreigners! "Look," I said to the Consul-General. "You were born in Stow-on-the-Wold and I was born in Egham. How can anyone born in Egham be a foreigner? We're British, British as they come, so how can we be foreigners?" "Yes," he said, "but to the Egyptians we're foreigners!" "Look," I said, "who's making the laws? Us or the Egyptians? We're making them, aren't we? So how can we be so daft as to make ourselves foreign? Especially when it's the Fayoum at stake."'

'Rules us out, doesn't it?' said Owen.

'Yes. From one of the provinces with the biggest economic potential. Crazy!'

'What makes it worse,' said Owen, 'is that the other people don't play fair.'

'That's it! You'd be amazed at the tricks they get up to. Buying shares under false names, entering into alliances with all sorts of unlikely people who claim to be Egyptians!'

'The Kfouri Brothers?'

'Notorious! Wouldn't touch them with a bargepole. Tried it once but they skin you alive. Fifty-fifty, you'd think, wouldn't you? But no, it had to be seventy-thirty, with them getting the seventy. "Nothing doing, old chap!" I said. "Fair is fair, and unless you give me a decent crack of the whip, you won't see my money!"'

'The trouble is, other people are not so scrupulous.'

'That's exactly it.'

'Tvardovsky, for instance?'

'Who knows what he got up to!'

'Especially in the Fayoum. In fact, I was wondering about that. He used to bank with you, didn't he?'

'He did,' said the Chairman, putting on his other tarboosh as Manager of the British Bank of the Levant.

'A bit of a surprise, that.'

'Not really. "I always bank with the best," he said. "Then people ask fewer questions."'

'Yes. He used to say other things as well. What I was wondering was whether your records could tell us anything about his dealings in the Fayoum.'

'What are you after?'

'Nature and extent.'

'Extent considerable, but we wouldn't have a complete picture. He used to bank with other people as well. As to nature –'

He looked doubtful.

'You might be able to get some idea, I suppose.'

'What I was particularly interested in,' said Owen, 'was his dealings through other people.'

'Such as?'

'The Kfouris?'

'He dealt *with* them, not through them. They are not the sort of people you deal through. And that was all a year or so ago. At one time he was very thick with them, but then they fell out.'

'Any idea why?'

The Chairman shrugged.

'Same reason as I fell out with them, I imagine,' he said. 'They tried to cut too deep. But that kind of thing doesn't show up in bank statements.'

'All right, not the Kfouris, then. But other people. Whose

names he used. Might not the statements give a clue to them? Cheques made out to them, banker's drafts?'

'It would be a lot of work,' said the Chairman doubtfully.

'It might be worth it. If it led to foreigners being kept out.'

'Ah, well, in that case –'

All through the day Owen kept expecting to hear from Mahmoud. No message came, however. Owen suspected that he had a fight on his hands. Ministries did not move. They didn't move much for Mamur Zapts with privileged access to the top; they didn't move at all for relatively junior Parquet officers.

Mahmoud would need all the help he could get, so it was a little surprising that he had not contacted Owen. Some help, though, was coming from the Nationalists. The newspapers that morning were full of the Strakhov case. *Al-Liwa* had spread it all over the front page. The other Arabic news-papers, all of whom were Nationalist, had given it almost equal prominence. If you were a Nationalist – and most of the officials, certainly in the Ministry of Justice were – it would be hard to miss it, which might give Mahmoud some of the support he needed.

The trouble was, the support would have to be mobilized. They had only forty-eight hours, of which nearly twenty-four had now elapsed. Perhaps that was what Mahmoud was doing – using his political contacts with the Nationalist Party to marshal support.

Owen was taking Zeinab out that evening. They had seen the opera at the main opera house, the Khedivial, so went to the smaller Abbas Theatre instead. It was a huge wooden barn of a building with benches at the front and boxes at the back, separated from each other by low, four-foot-high partitions. Many had harem grilles.

In the box next to theirs a dinner-jacketed man was sitting by himself.

'Hello, Owen,' said Prince Fuad.

'Hello, Prince! I didn't realize you were an opera devotee.'

'I'm not,' said Fuad, 'but I am a devotee of the donna.'

The prima donna, newly arrived in Cairo, was young and slim – unusual, this, in prima donnas – and strikingly beautiful.

'And can she sing, too?'

'Don't know about that,' said Fuad indifferently.

He looked at Zeinab curiously. Owen introduced her.

'Nuri Pasha's daughter? Well, I know Nuri, of course, but I never knew –'

A waiter arrived bringing champagne.

'Two more glasses,' said the Prince. 'Oh, and don't forget: a bottle afterwards in the dressing room.'

He took a sip and then put the glass down on the little table beside him.

'Well,' he said, 'how goes the hunt?'

'Slowly. We keep meeting obstacles.'

'Like a steeplechase,' said the Prince with relish. 'Damned good fun!'

He took another sip.

'Still, you need to get a move on,' he said, frowning. 'I can't go for too long without my certificates. I hope you're remembering?'

'I certainly am. I regard them as very important.'

'Good,' said the Prince, slightly surprised but pleased. 'Good! Let me fill you up.'

He put down the bottle.

'What about these obstacles? Anything I can do? A boot up somebody's backside? Glad to help.'

'No backsides need booting just at the moment, thanks,' said Owen.

A thought suddenly struck him.

'Except –'

'Yes?'

'There *is* something you might possibly be able to help on. But I hardly like to ask. It's very, very tricky.'

126

'A challenge, eh?' said Fuad, getting interested.

'It certainly is. The fact is, there's a man we're very anxious to talk to. Only we can't gain access to him.'

'Soon see about that!' said Fuad.

'He's in prison. And he's being deported tomorrow.'

'Undesirable, is he?'

'Very probably. But he might know something that would help us in getting hold of your certificates.'

'Name?' said Fuad.

'Strakhov. But, look, there are powerful bodies involved. Ministries —'

'Ministers?' said Fuad. 'I eat them.'

'Foreign countries —'

'Kick them in the balls.'

'Russia —'

'Especially.'

'Only it's got to be done tomorrow.'

'Sure, sure. First thing.' The Prince suddenly looked anxious. 'Actually,' he said, 'possibly not first thing. I'll be with Silvie until eleven.'

'Does that leave you enough time?'

'Oh, yes. She's got to go to rehearsals then anyway.'

As soon as he saw Mahmoud, Owen knew that something had happened.

'You've not got anywhere?'

'No. It's not that. Not exactly.'

Mahmoud sat down in the seat opposite. He had rung Owen about halfway through the morning asking to see him.

'What is it, then?'

'They've explained,' said Mahmoud, 'why they wouldn't act.'

'Well?'

'They've got bigger fish to fry.'

'Such as?'

'The Capitulations.'

'The Capitulations!'

'Part of them, at least.'

'What is this?'

'There's a case coming up,' said Mahmoud. 'It's to do with where a company is registered.'

'De Vries and Boutigny,' said Owen.

'You know about it?' said Mahmoud, surprised.

'Well, I wouldn't say I entirely understand it –'

'It's very important. At the moment, you see, a company which is to all intents and purposes Egyptian – all its business is in Egypt, its board meetings are held in Egypt, and so on – can register abroad and so escape the obligations of Egyptian company law. In particular it escapes a requirement to deposit a quarter of its proposed capital before it can be allowed to operate – a necessary requirement at this stage in Egypt's economic development. Well, the Court of First Instance has just ruled that any company formed in this way for the purpose of evading Egyptian company law is null and nonexistent. It is a major ruling,' said Mahmoud enthusiastically, 'a tremendous assertion of Egyptian sovereignty!'

'And the Ministry supports it?'

'It certainly does!'

'But why should that affect the Strakhov case?'

'Because they don't want to rock the boat. It's still got to go to appeal and there could be a lot of pressure, from the Capitulatory Powers especially, to reverse it. They can't afford to antagonize Russia just at this point.'

'It's so important that everything else has to be sacrificed to it?'

'That's right.'

'Strakhov?'

Mahmoud nodded.

'That,' he said, 'is just the point.'

He sat silently for a moment. Then he said:

'I knew about the case, of course. I knew that it was important. But what I had not seen was this angle.' He looked at Owen. 'In the Ministry,' he said, 'they believe that policy and politics are not for juniors. So I hadn't taken it in.'

Owen was silent, too. It was certainly something that he had not taken in, either. But then, law, like finance, was an area he tended to leave to specialists.

'You think they're right?' he said.

'I think it makes sense, yes, to try not to antagonize the Powers in the run-up to the appeal.'

He was silent again.

'This is very important, you see,' he said, after a moment. 'We don't want to run any risk of it going wrong.'

'No.'

'Besides,' he said, looking at Owen as if he was expecting – indeed, provoking – him to disagree, 'Strakhov is not even an Egyptian.'

'True.'

'The general good must take priority over the individual good.'

'I daresay,' said Owen.

Mahmoud sighed.

'But –' he said.

10

'De Vries and Boutigny: know about it?'

'Only too well. If for no other reason,' said Paul, 'than that Jarvis rings me up about it at least every other day. It's coming up for appeal on the twenty-ninth.'

'Paul, what is our attitude towards it? As an Administration, I mean?'

'All for it.'

'Really?'

'What do you mean: "really"?'

'Well, I thought the Old Man might not be – that he might want the appeal to succeed. British interests and all that.'

'The Old Man's all for it. Been lobbying for it ever since he got here.'

'Really?'

'Gareth, why all this "really"?'

'Well, it's bound up with the Capitulations, isn't it? I know that we're not, as an Administration, all that keen on the Capitulations but I thought that was only because we didn't want the other powers to have the privileges. It never occurred to me that we might not want them for ourselves.'

'Ah, but you're forgetting the point of the whole exercise. What the British are here for, why a British Administration was set up in the first place, was to sort out Egypt's finances.'

'But I thought –?'

'I know. The last thing you would have thought was that they actually would try and sort out Egypt's finances. But look at it this way: what, at bottom, is the Old Man?'

'Well –'

'Apart from being a bastard. I'll tell you. He's a banker. So was Cromer before him. And once a banker, always a banker. So when they got put here they behaved like bankers. They cut this and they chopped that, raised this and increased that. They actually did what they were supposed to do. We British are like that. Sometimes. Other countries never know where they are with us. That's why they call us the perfidious British.'

'But –'

'Anyway, they were as happy as sandboys, cutting this and raising that, until they came up against the Capitulations and found that they were stopping them from doing these fine things. So Cromer said: "The Capitulations have got to go!" In fact, it wasn't the Capitulations that went, but him. And then the Old Man came out here and he's been saying the same thing.'

'But, Paul, what's all that got to do with De Vries and Boutigny? Surely they're not strictly part of the Capitulations. I know they're bound up with it somehow, but surely, strictly –'

'But that is precisely the point. Does it come under the Capitulations or does it not? That's exactly what the Court of Appeal has to decide. There are some Powers that think it does. We think it doesn't. If it doesn't, the Egyptian courts are free to rule on businesses operating under Egyptian company law.'

'So in this the Old Man's following Egyptian interests not British interests?'

'You could say that.'

'Well, I'm damned! You mean that in this we're on the side of the Nationalists?'

'I am sure that, with your usual elasticity, you will be able to cope.'

Owen was silent for a minute, reflecting. Then he said:

'So that's why the Old Man was unwilling to twist arms over Strakhov?'

'You'd think that when you were twisting so many, a few

more wouldn't make much difference; but, broadly, yes. Russia is one of the powers that are being difficult and he sees no point in making things worse just at the moment. Once the appeal is out of the way, then, yes, he'd be only too delighted to refuse Russia extradition or, indeed, anything else.'

'By that time, though, Strakhov will be back in Russia.'

Paul shrugged.

'Little things, I'm afraid, have to give way to big. I've done what I could. Mahmoud has forty-eight hours' grace, thanks to the Admiralty. It's up to him now. If he can persuade the Ministries, the Old Man won't intervene.'

'But, Paul, they're all behind the Old Man on a thing like this.'

'What do you expect? This is important to Egypt.'

'The Ministries won't budge,' said Mahmoud wearily. 'Even my own Ministry. They say, we've been fighting for this for years. Now, at last, unless something goes wrong, it's going to happen. We're going to make damned sure that nothing goes wrong.'

'You can understand their point of view.'

'Of course I can understand their point of view!' exploded Mahmoud. 'I share it. I ask myself why I am bothering about Strakhov at all. Or about Tvardovsky, come to that. They're just individual cases. But this – this question of the Capitulation is something much bigger. It touches on the whole question of the standing of Egypt, it is about Egypt, Egypt! So why am I holding back? Why, why?'

'You're not holding back! You're as keen as they are. It's just that at the same time you're also pursuing –'

'I know, I know! That is what I say to myself. What I say to them. But do you know what they say to me? Or if they do not say it, they think it: Mahmoud, you are a traitor!'

'No, no, come on –'

'Yes!'

Mahmoud beat his chest dramatically.

'That is what they think. This man, they say, when all

should be pulling together, goes off and chases butterflies! Because that is what it is. Strakhov is a butterfly, a mere butterfly, compared to this. Worse; because of this, this mere butterfly, things could go wrong.'

'Oh, come. Look, the Russians are not going to let their attitude towards De Vries and Boutigny be affected by a tiny sideshow like Strakhov!'

'You think so? But, let me tell you, these powers are jealous of their privileges. For Strakhov as a man they care nothing. Pah! He is a mere insect. But for their privileges, yes, they care a lot. And one privilege is bound up with another. That is what the Capitulations system *is*!'

He stared fiercely at Owen; as if, for a moment, he was the personal embodiment of the Capitulations system. Which, of course, in a sense, he was.

'That is why Strakhov is important. They will say, this is an attack on our privileges. And this De Vries and Boutigny business is another one. The De Vries and Boutigny we could perhaps put up with. We can see there are arguments. But now this Strakhov business comes along and it is like – it is like a last straw! And what my friends say is this: "Mahmoud," they said, "why have you got to lay on this last straw? Why is this Strakhov so important to you?" And, I, too, I ask myself, why is Strakhov so important to me, why?'

He looked at Owen dramatically.

'I'll tell you,' said Owen. 'It is because you are a good lawyer.'

'A good lawyer,' said Mahmoud bitterly, 'but a bad Egyptian!'

All at once he seemed to crumple. He sat there silently for some time, brooding. A waiter brought more coffee but he ignored it. Owen, used to his violent swings of mood, waited.

'Do you know what I have spent the morning doing?' Mahmoud said after a while. 'I have spent it talking to politicians. I have some contacts through the Nationalist Party. Well, I have been speaking to them. "This is an abuse of the system," I say, "which must be put right." "It must,

Mahmoud," they agree. "An individual's rights are being disregarded," I say. They look grave. "So can you help me?" I say. "Mahmoud, we would if we could, but –" they say. "But what?" I say. "Mahmoud, there are bigger things at stake." "An individual's rights," I say. "They are deporting him illegally." "Mahmoud," they say, "which is the more important to you? Egypt, or this foreigner?" "The law," I say. "The law is what is important to me. And if it is not applied justly everywhere, even to an insect foreigner, then Egypt itself is weakened." "Mahmoud," they say, shaking their heads, "what world is this that you live in?"'

'It is too late to do anything now,' said Owen.

'No,' said Mahmoud. 'There is one other thing to try.'

He stood up.

'I am going to see Mirza es-Rahel,' he said. 'If the law can do nothing, then perhaps the press can. This,' he said bitterly, 'is the world we live in.'

Nikos, Owen's official clerk, was comfortable with paper, less at ease with people. What he would have made of Mahmoud this morning Owen could not think. But what he had made of the company files in the Registry was a lot more than Owen had.

He laid some sheets of paper before him.

'This is the list of shareholders in the Fayoum Light Railway Company,' he said. 'You will remember that shareholding was restricted to native Egyptians. The clerk in the registry has been checking how far this turned out to be so. He has put a cross besides those who are clearly not native Egyptians. The chief problem, however, is shares that are held in Egyptian names but almost certainly owned in reality by foreign investors. Now –'

He directed Owen to another sheet.

'This is a list of shareholders in the Covered Markets Company. You will see that there is considerable overlap.'

He put another sheet before Owen.

'This is a list of shareholders in other companies in the

Fayoum. You will see again that there is considerable over-lap.'

'Wouldn't you expect Fayoum people to invest in Fayoum companies?'

'I'm not sure that I would. How many people are there in the Fayoum with money to invest? In particular, how many people are there with the money to invest in this company and that company and that –? We have checked some of the names that recur against census data. It is remarkable how many quite humble people in Medinet have really consider-able holdings of shares.'

'So you're saying that somebody has been building up ownership under other people's names?'

'That is right. Now, I have also checked the names against data that Tvardovsky's bank has supplied and in a number of the cases there is quite clearly a connection. Cheques have been made out to them, drawn on Tvardovsky's account, and there have also been a lot of bearer's orders. You must remember that many of these people, the ones in Medinet especially, do not have bank accounts. The orders are always for relatively small sums. Now, of course, with bearer's orders it is not possible to identify names, although the bank clerks at Medinet may well be able to remember some of the people who have tendered them, especially if they are not people who normally have anything to do with the bank.'

'You think Tvardovsky was paying them cash for the use of their names?'

'Yes. And you should be able to check this. Tvardovsky will almost certainly have wished to hold the share certificates himself, which means that they should be somewhere among his effects.'

He turned to go, triumphant. Nikos, too, had theories about the real world. It was a shadowy, exciting construct made of paper, of which the world of physical objects and people was a tedious reflection. Paper was where the exciting things hap-pened, where real, dark secrets of the universe were revealed. Tvardovsky, he had decided, was a man after his own heart.

'You know,' he said, 'you have to admire him. At the time he was stopped, he was well on his way to buying up the whole of the Fayoum.'

Long mornings – Owen was awake at five, in his office by six and didn't lunch till two – short afternoons (siesta for some) and long, dawdling evenings, that was the Cairo pattern of life. It was two o'clock now and he had arranged to meet Zeinab for lunch. He took an arabeah up to the Ismailiya quarter, got out at the Midan Suleiman Basha, glanced down the Sharia el Antikkahaneh el Masriyeh to where the Nile glistened in the sun and then set out along one of the side streets behind the Savoy Hotel.

The street happened to be the one in which Raoul's art gallery was, set there to take advantage, he hoped, of the tourists. It was a modern shop with a glass-fronted window and in the window were two paintings. Owen stopped to look at them as he went by.

'An expert appraisal?' said a voice behind him.

It was Yussuf, one of the artists he had met at the reception.

'What do you think of them?'

'I think,' said Yussuf, 'that Raoul has put them in the window precisely because it doesn't matter if the sun spoils them.'

Owen laughed.

'You artists!' he said. 'You're always catty about each other.'

'And we shouldn't be, I know,' sighed Yussuf. 'Who is there to speak for us when we can't even speak well of each other?'

They walked along the street together, keeping, by mutual consent, to the shade.

'On days like this,' said Yussuf, 'I sometimes think I would like to be a landscape painter. Preferably in the Fayoum.'

'Like Natasha?'

'*Not* like Natasha. Natasha is an amateur. Bother, there I go again, disparaging a fellow artist. Except that Natasha isn't really an artist. But I still shouldn't disparage her. Not everyone has a good eye.'

'She has a good eye, has she?'

'Oh, yes. Less for paintings, perhaps, than for objects. That's how she makes her living, you know.'

'Makes her living? I thought that maybe Savinkov –'

'Oh, Savinkov looks after her. Perhaps I should say: that's how she makes her pocket money.'

'By –?'

'Selling on objects.'

'What sort of objects?'

'Well, perhaps I shouldn't say this, but antique objects. Usually not big enough to require an export permit, small stuff that is picked up locally and she gets from her friends in the Fayoum. You know that old Russian lady? She has contacts everywhere: with the archaeologists, with the shopkeepers, with the headmaster, even, who, I believe, is a particularly valuable source.'

'And Natasha sells them on? To people like Raoul?'

'People like. Not Raoul. I don't think Raoul would bother himself with small stuff. Pottery, beads, that sort of thing.'

'He was asking me about a mummy portrait, you know, like that one he had in his exhibition.'

'Well, of course, that would be very valuable and he might well be interested in that. But that would, I imagine, require a permit. Unless it was in fragments.' He looked at Owen. 'You know about fragments?'

'Tell me.'

'Well, the Department of Antiquities doesn't usually bother about fragments. There are so many of them. In some places in Egypt you walk on them as you go about your daily business. Fragments of mummy cases, pottery. So a dealer can usually get away with exporting them. But then, when they get to their destination, they are fitted together again.'

'And Natasha does *that*?'

'I don't think she actually breaks them, if that's what you mean. She cares about them too much for that. But I think that what she looks for particularly are good examples of broken work, a mummy case, say, or a portrait, where the pieces, or most of them, survive. She is, you could say, a specialist.'

They had come to the restaurant now and Owen could see Zeinab waiting inside. She saw Yussuf and waved a hand. Owen took him in and suggested he join them in an aperitif.

'Well, perhaps fruit juice,' conceded the artist.

He sat down.

'Yes' he said, 'she's quite a specialist in her way.'

'Specialist?' said Zeinab. 'Who?'

'Natasha.'

'Natasha again?' said Zeinab, turning towards Owen.

It was evening: the moment when the city woke up again after its siesta and became alive. The sun had gone off the streets leaving it just pleasantly warm. The sharp contrasts between light and shadow had disappeared, leaving a soft duskiness out of which people emerged without assertiveness. The stridency of the city during the day was suddenly muted. Everyone became gentler. Arabeah drivers no longer forced their way through the streets, the heavy carts had stopped altogether.

As the lamps came on in the cafés the tables outside began to fill up with young effendis. In the side streets off the squares doors opened and children and women came out to sit on the steps. Sometimes a smell of fried onions drifted out from inside.

The main thoroughfares like the Mouski filled with evening promenaders sauntering along looking into the glass windows of the shops. From inside, behind the counters on which the shopkeepers sat, came smells of spices and new leather, mingling, near the squares, with the sharper aromas of coffee and burnt peanuts.

It was a moment of the day that Owen loved. He collected tomorrow's newspapers from his office and wandered out

138

into the streets, coming to rest, as he always did, at the café in the Musshi.

It was where people knew they could find him and as he sat there, sipping his coffee, various people dropped into the seat opposite him for a few quiet words: a fat Greek, for example, who stayed for some time, the sweat spreading damp patches under his armpits, one or two nondescript men in galabeahs, even a donkey-boy. It was the time-honoured place for business in Egypt – not these great blocks like the Credit Lyonnais or the Office of the Public Debt – and for many of his agents a more comfortable place to come than his office at the Bab-el-Khalk.

He took up a copy of *Al-Liwa* and looked at the front page. Then, puzzled, he opened it and searched inside. Nowhere could he find even a mention of Strakhov. Sure he had missed it, he went through again. There was nothing.

He picked up the other papers. There was no reference to Strakhov in them, either. Well, perhaps that was not surprising. But that there should be nothing in *Al-Liwa*!

He checked through the papers again, put them down, and sipped his coffee.

Not long afterwards, Mahmoud, who also knew where to find him, came threading his way through the tables towards him. His face was expressionless.

Owen tapped the newspapers. Mahmoud nodded.

'I tried,' he said.

'And they wouldn't –?'

'They took the same line as the Ministries. I spoke to es-Rahel. He said they were afraid that it might prejudice other issues.'

The waiter came and poured him some coffee.

'So –?' said Owen.

Mahmoud shrugged.

'So,' he said.

'Too late to do anything now,' said Owen.

'Yes.'

They sat for a while in silence.

'What now?' asked Owen.

Mahmoud shrugged again.

'Back to Tvardovsky. Strakhov was only one lead among others.'

'He probably couldn't have told us much anyway.'

'It was not what he had to tell that was important,' said Mahmoud. 'It is what they are doing to him.'

'Yes.'

He could see Mahmoud slipping into depression. To distract him, he told him what Nikos had found out. Mahmoud listened but without interest. His mind was still on Strakhov.

'You've done what you could,' said Owen.

Mahmoud shrugged defeatedly.

'Too late now, anyway.'

Through the tables came a beaming man dressed in the livery of the Savoy Hotel.

'Effendi!' he cried.

'Yes?' said Owen, startled.

'They said I would find you here!'

'If it is the Mamur Zapt you search for, it is the Mamur Zapt that you have found.'

'It is the Mamur Zapt that I search for. Effendi, there is a message for you. It is from Prince Fuad. He wishes to speak to you.'

'Where is he?'

'In Alexandria.'

'Alexandria!'

'Yes, Effendi, but he would speak with you by telephone. He rang your office, but – Effendi, these are his words, not mine – the idle sods had all gone home. So he rang the Savoy and told them to send someone out to find you.'

'What's the Savoy there for?' said the Prince dismissively. 'And, anyway, since you hadn't got a telephone of your own –'

'Prince, I'm always glad to answer the phone to you anywhere, but –'

'Rang them up,' said Fuad. 'Rang them up as soon as Silvie left. About twelve o'clock. A bit later than I had expected. She's a stronger girl than I thought. Anyway, rang them up, as I said. But got nowhere. So I thought, this won't do, dammit, said I'd do something. So I drove down there –'

'Drove down? To Alexandria?'

'Yes. Nothing like talking man to man. Besides, time was short. It was already two o'clock by this time (had to have lunch, old chap – or was it breakfast?) so I knew I had to get a move on. So I drove down. Fast. Got two brace.'

'Brace?'

'Of sand grouse. Hit them as they were crossing the road. And a dog, but that doesn't count. Nor the donkey.'

'You hit a donkey?'

'And a cart. Donkey's all right, cart not too good, though. Nor the man.'

'Prince –'

'Slowed me up. Still, got there in time. "Can't do this," I said. "Can't be sending chaps hither and thither. Especially to Russia. At least, not without my say-so. I want him out."'

'Out?'

'Don't trust officials. Never know what they might do. Safer to have charge myself. Interesting chap. Rings birds. At least, he did when he was in Russia. Shot one once myself, on my estate. A crane. There was this ring around its leg, attached to a cylinder about the size of a cartridge case. Inside, there was a note, to say the crane had been ringed in South Russia. Interesting, that, isn't it? Long way, for a bird. And turned up on my estate! Can't be much wrong with a chap who sends birds to my estate.'

'Prince, we are talking about Strakhov?'

'Who else did you think I was talking about?'

'And you've got him out? Out of prison?'

'Yes.'

'Prince, where exactly is he? Now?'

'Here. I've got a place near Alexandria. Why don't you come down?'

11

A carriage was waiting for them when they got off the train at a stop just before Damanhur. It took them through fields of durra and, later, lentils and barley, until ahead of them they saw orange groves and, to one side, the palm trees of a village. They turned up through the orange trees and came to a courtyard with a long low house on one side and outbuildings on the others. In one corner of the court-yard there was a threshing floor, where a small boy was driving a pair of buffaloes over the cut corn on a wooden, harrow-like implement with what looked like a lot of circular knives.

A raised verandah ran along the front of the house and on it two men were sitting having breakfast: Prince Fuad and a tall, thin man on whom a suit hung loosely. Fuad came down the steps to greet them.

'He doesn't shoot,' he confided to Owen.

'Well, no.'

'Pity, that. You'd have thought a chap interested in birds –'

He led the way up on to the verandah. Strakhov shook hands shyly.

'Leave you,' said Prince Fuad, and stalked off. A little later Owen saw him going into the orange trees with a .22.

They sat down at the table with the used breakfast things. A servant came and took them away.

'What am I doing here?' said Strakhov.

He seemed utterly bewildered.

It was not an easy question to answer and Mahmoud did not try. Instead, he said:

'I am the Parquet officer investigating Tvardovsky's death and there are some things I want to ask you.'

'Tvardovsky! Investigating?' The Russian seemed stunned for a moment. 'So,' he said then, slowly, 'it wasn't an accident!'

'That is for us still a question.'

The man was silent for a while. Then he said:

'No, no, you are right. I see that now. I did wonder at the time but I thought, I thought Tvardovsky is big, they will not reach for him. It is not the big fish they go for, but the small. Like me,' he said bitterly. 'So when they said it was an accident I believed them. Even though he had told me.'

'He had told you?'

'He knew. One day he came into the home – I run a home for seamen – and I could tell that he was frightened. I said to him: "What is the matter, Alexei?" And he said: "They have found out, and now they will try to kill me." I said to him: "What nonsense is this, Alexei? Why should they try to kill you?" "They will think I have tricked them," he said. "Well, in a way I have. But it is not as they suppose." "Then talk to them, Alexei," I said. "Tell them it is not as they think." "Oh, they will not listen," he said. And, of course he was right. One does not reason with the bear. "You must run away," I said. "You must run away at once!" "No," he said. "There is still a chance. If they see that there's nothing they can do about it, then perhaps they will let it rest. There are other things for them to swallow, after all." And after that he did not speak about it, and I thought, well, perhaps it had just been a bad day, and if he could forget about it, then I could. So I thought no more about it, even when he died. But now I see,' said Strakhov, 'that they reach out in the end. Even for the big fish. That is what they always tell you. "The Tsar's arm is long," they say, "and he never forgets."'

'What had Tvardovsky done,' asked Owen, 'that the Tsar should reach out for him?'

Strakhov hesitated.

'I do not know what he had done. I know only that the Tsar's reach is long.'

'But he must have done something,' said Owen, 'for the Tsar to reach out for him.'

'He helped people. Others beside me. There was a woman he worked with. She used to help to get people out, people who were wanted by the Okhrana. There were a lot of us after the strike. She used to go to places like Istanbul and Budapest and wait for people there. She used to pretend that she was selling art objects, antiques – she was able to get hold of them partly through Tvardovsky, partly through a friend they had in the Fayoum.'

'And you think that perhaps the Okhrana –?'

'There is a man at the Consulate who works for the Okhrana. He had begun to be around a lot, always asking questions. And after Tvardovsky died, he came and searched his rooms –'

'Just a moment,' said Owen. 'How do you know it was him?'

'One of the seamen saw him. He knew him, of course, we know all those men. His name is Tobin –'

'Tobin?' said Owen.

'Yes. He came to warn me. Tobin had policemen with him and we thought they would be coming next to us. Well, they didn't. Not that day. It was two days later that they came and took me away.'

Some way off, among the orange trees, there was the crack of a shot. Owen met Prince Fuad as he was coming back to the house. He was carrying two dead pigeons.

'Pigeons!' he said disgustedly, showing them to Owen. 'That's all there is round here. I think I must get away for some proper shooting. To the Fayoum, perhaps.'

*   *   *

144

Mahmoud took Strakhov back to Cairo with him on the next train. Owen caught the train in the other direction, going to Alexandria. There he went to call on Messieurs Demetriades and Atiyah. Yes, they said, as a matter of fact there were a number of share certificates among Tvardovsky's effects.

Could Owen see them?

Demetriades looked at Atiyah and Atiyah looked at Demetriades.

'Other people have asked that,' said Demetriades.

'And we have said no,' said Atiyah.

'However –'

Among the titles to ownership were several in names that he recognized. Prince Fuad was one. Irena Kundasova was another. Sayid Al-Akham was another. Sayid Al-Akham? Of course, that was the headmaster. And what was this? Among the share certificates were titles to land also, many of them. What was the name, now? Abdullah. Yes, in the titles to land was one in the name of Abdullah Farkit – the old man previously in possession of the parcel of land where Pharaohs had so fortunately shat.

The holding in Irena Kundasova's name was particularly large. Owen thought for a moment and then turned to the lawyers.

'The effect of the will is to return these certificates to Irena Kundasova, is it not?'

'It should certainly do that.'

'What about the others?'

'That,' said Demetriades, 'is an interesting question. Legally, I mean. There is, naturally, a presumption that the shares belong to the people in whose names they are made out. However, if they have been lodged as security against sums paid out, then the estate could claim that, in default of the sums being repaid, ownership reverts to the estate.'

'But then,' said Owen, 'if there are doubts about the basis of the whole transaction –'

The eyebrows of Demetriades and Atiyah shot up.

'Doubts?'

'Legal ones, I mean.'

'Legal?'

The eyebrows shot still higher.

'Come on,' said Owen, 'you know what he was at. Some of these are shares in the Fayoum Light Railway Company, in which the ownership of shares is restricted to native Egyptians.'

'Oh, yes?'

'And others are in the Covered Markets Company, where at one time there was thought to be a high chance of a similar restriction.'

'Oh?'

'Come on,' said Owen. 'He was trying to get round the restriction, wasn't he?'

'Well, yes,' said Demetriades, after a moment.

'And yet –' said Atiyah.

'You make it sound as if it was just a deliberate breach of the law!' said Demetriades.

'Well, wasn't it?'

'Ye-es,' said Demetriades unwillingly.

'And no,' cut in Atiyah.

'It was a defensive manoeuvre,' said Demetriades.

'And not on his own behalf,' said Atiyah.

'Indeed not,' concurred Demetriades. 'It was to save the companies from being illicitly taken over.'

'You could say – in fact, I would argue this strongly in court – that our client's intention was not to pervert justice but to see that it was maintained.'

'Well, that *would* be a novel defence,' said Owen.

He came out into the Place Mohammed Ali, with its great statue, and turned left towards the Bourse, where he had been told he would find Savinkov. The Bourse was in an old mansion, the Palais Tossiza, which had once belonged to a Greek merchant and which had now been divided into the corn exchange at one end and the stock exchange at the other. Both exchanges had closed now but dealers were still sitting in the cafés outside.

Savinkov must have been watching out for him, for as Owen approached, he got up and came towards him. They found an empty table some way away from the others and sat down.

'Mr Savinkov,' said Owen, 'were you one of the people helping Natasha and Tvardovsky to get revolutionaries out of Russia?'

'How do you know about that?'

'Through Strakhov.'

Savinkov shrugged.

'I just provided money.'

'You weren't part of the organization?'

'No.'

'Was Tvardovsky?'

'No. There wasn't really an organization. It was just a few individuals, Natasha mostly, but they could call on the support of the seamen's union.'

'Nevertheless, you contributed. Tell me, Mr Savinkov, did you have any fear that because of that the Okhrana might one day reach out for you?'

The Russian seemed surprised.

'No,' he said.

'As it reached out for Tvardovsky?'

'Did Strakhov say that? He is talking nonsense. The Okhrana has better things to do. The trouble with Strakhov – as it is with many who have suffered under the Tsar, Natasha also – is that he thinks the Okhrana is still pursuing him.'

'Well, isn't it?'

'Strakhov, perhaps,' Savinkov conceded. 'But Tvardovsky? No.'

'And yet a member of the Okhrana was asking questions about Tvardovsky in the days before he died.'

'Was he?'

'Yes. And he ransacked Tvardovsky's room after he died.'

'Did he?'

'Tobin,' said Owen.

'Oh.'

'I don't think this comes as any surprise to you, Mr Savinkov,' said Owen.

'Possibly not.'

'I think he was also the European Effendi who searched Irena Kundasova's house.'

'That *did* surprise me,' said Savinkov. 'A little.'

'But not much?'

'I had my suspicions.'

'Irena Kundasova knew he was a Russian and thought he was from the Third Section. Of course, he was not from the Third Section but from the Okhrana. But was he working for the Okhrana, Mr Savinkov, when he broke into Irena Kundasova's house?'

'Possibly not,' said Savinkov, after a moment.

'Or when he searched Tvardovsky's rooms?'

'That is more questionable. But probably not then, either.'

'Then who was he working for, Mr Savinkov? I ask you, knowing that you were a friend of Tvardovsky's.'

'That, Captain Owen, you must leave to others,' said Savinkov, getting up from the table. 'Knowing that they were Tvardovsky's friends.'

Back in Cairo the next morning, Owen was arranging his and Zeinab's holiday weekend in the Fayoum. That took some doing. The hotel by the lake did not have a telephone; nor did its mother hotel in Medinet; nor, it appeared almost, did anyone else in the Fayoum.

'For Christ's sake!' expostulated Owen.

'We haven't got there yet,' said the official defensively.

'Where have you got?'

'We've got trunk lines to Alexandria and Port Said and one or two other places are on the system.'

'The Fayoum?'

'Not the Fayoum. Important places. Like where my mother lives.'

'The Fayoum *is* an important place. There's a lot of development going on there –'

'The Fayoum?' said the official, mock-innocently. 'Where's that?'

'Try State Telegraphs,' advised Nikos.

The State Telegraph service formed part of the railway administration and at first it was the same story there.

'The Fayoum?' said the official doubtfully. 'I don't think we've got an office there. Why don't you telegraph somewhere else?'

'Look,' said Owen, 'you're part of the railways. The Fayoum's got railways. Surely you can get in touch with them?'

'Well –'

'The Fayoum Light Railway Company,' said Owen, with a flash of inspiration. 'Why don't you try them?'

Impressed, the official picked up the message. Then he hesitated.

'But how is it going to get from their offices to the hotel?'

'You're going to ask them to send on the message by bearer. And you're going to tell them that if it doesn't get there the Mamur Zapt is going to come down in person and devise excrutiating torments for them!'

The manager of the office, a short, round, cherry-faced Egyptian, stuck his head in at that point.

'Having trouble?'

'I'm just trying to send a telegram to the Fayoum!'

'That shouldn't be difficult. We have a local arrangement with a company there. Here, let me have it. I'll see it gets through.'

He came into the room and took the slip from his subordinate.

'The Fayoum's a rapidly developing area,' said Owen, mollified. 'I'm surprised you haven't got your own office there.'

'We will have. In fact, it will be one of the biggest in the country – a really exciting project,' said the manager

149

enthusiastically. 'You're right: the Fayoum is a developing area. And a service like this would make a big difference to it. I think people can see this already – you'd be amazed at the amount of interest there is down there! We've had so many tenders, you wouldn't believe –'

'Tenders?' said Owen.

'Yes. For construction and installation.'

'Do you have the names of the tenderers?'

'I have the tenders themselves. In fact, I was just going through them when –'

'Could I have a look at them?'

He followed the manager into his office. On his desk was a large open file containing a bundle of papers. Owen picked up the top set.

'Breithorst.' He turned the pages over. 'Where are they registered?'

'Berlin, I think.'

'Leblanc Construction?'

'Paris.'

'Jones and Waring – no need to ask. Cowie and Macdonald. Mactavity Cement. Richards Grant –'

He laid the papers down.

'Any Egyptians?'

'Well, there are the Kfouri Brothers, of course.'

With the main business of the day, main, that is, so far as he was concerned – getting their holiday booked – accomplished, Owen returned to his office. The next day's newspapers were beginning to come in. Prominent among them – and unusually early – was *Al-Liwa*. Nikos had put it on top of the pile and marked one item heavily with a blue pencil. Owen picked it up and read the item.

It referred to a recent high-handed action of a member of the royal family noted for his intemperate conduct. He had, it appeared, personally intervened and extricated from custody a man held quite legitimately – who was, in fact, facing extradition – and gone off with him. Was such imperiousness to be endured, the newspaper thundered? Did the royal family think it was still living in the days of Mohammed Ali? How did it imagine such behaviour was viewed by those – and there were many of them in Egypt – who believed in the principles of liberal constitutionalism? To say nothing about how it would look to our international friends – something that was especially important at this particularly critical time!

If the news was coming out in tomorrow's *Al-Liwa*, the other newspapers would already have it, too. Ho-hum, thought Owen, and sat back to await developments.

They were not long in coming.

First, an agitated phone call came from the prison administration at Alexandria.

'Captain Owen, a strange – a dreadful! – thing has happened!'

'Good heavens! What is it?'

'A man has escaped from one of our prisons!'

'Escaped?'

'Well, not exactly escaped . . .'

There was a long silence.

'The fact is, Captain Owen, that someone came in and took him out.'

'Took him out? But, surely –'

'The difficulty is, Captain Owen,' said the voice unhappily, 'that it was a prince of the blood.'

'Well, that is very difficult. However, I don't see why you are ringing me.'

'We need to find this man at once. The Russian Consul –'

'I suggest you speak to the Alexandria Police,' said Owen happily.

A little later the phone rang again. It was Mathews, the Head of the Alexandria Police Force. He sounded oddly diffident.

'Owen, got a spot of bother here. Wondered if you could help. Fact is, a chap's got out of one of our prisons. Well, not exactly got out. Was taken out. By one of the royal princes.'

'Hm,' said Owen. 'High up, eh? Sounds bad. When you've been in this country as long as I have, you find that some things have a bit of a smell. I suggest you get on to the Minister.'

Not the Minister, but a Deputy Minister rang up next.

'Nothing to do with me,' said Owen, remembering the run-around Mahmoud had been given in Alexandria. 'Why don't you try the Ministry of Justice?'

And when the Ministry of Justice rang up, he said:

'No, no, I'm nothing to do with any of this. They've kept me out. Why don't you try the Ministry of the Interior?'

This time it was Henderson, the Adviser, who rang up.

'I can't speak for the royal family,' said Owen, enjoying this. 'You'll have to get on to the Khedive's office.'

It was not long before the Khedive's office was on the phone.

'Try speaking to Prince Fuad,' he said.

'We have,' said the man from the Khedive's office. There was a short silence. 'It was not very productive,' he said.

'Dear, dear!'

'But he did say that if there were any questions, they should be put to you.'

This was a bit of a poser.

'There are a lot of questions, certainly. But I don't think they should be put to me. Try putting them to the Minister of the Interior, for a start.'

'It is all very odd,' said the man from the Khedive's office, puzzled. He hesitated. 'Could you tell me just what is Strakhov's connection with the British Navy?'

'The British Navy!'

'Yes. Apparently the British Admiralty has been much involved –'

And then Henderson rang again.

'Come on,' he said. 'We know you've got him.'

'Oh, but I'm holding him legally,' said Owen. 'On grounds of security.'

*   *   *

152

It was perhaps this that prompted a call in person from a senior member of the Russian Consulate.

'We understand that you are holding one of our nationals.'

'Don't worry,' Owen assured him. 'Due process will be followed. He will be brought before a court and given legal representation. That is, if you wish to bring any charges against him.'

'We are applying for extradition.'

'Fine!' said Owen. 'It will be all right to use the ordinary channels.'

The Consulate official drummed on the table with his fingers.

'We were hoping to dispense with that.'

'Surely not?'

'The Capitulations –'

'Make no mention of such dispensation. However,' said Owen carelessly, 'that is a legal matter and quite beyond me. It will have to be decided by the courts.'

The official sat thinking.

'By the way,' said Owen, 'what is the nature of Russia's interest in the Fayoum?'

'In the Fayoum?' said the official, startled. 'I don't think we have one.'

'I came across one of your staff doing research into companies in the Fayoum, that's all.'

The official shrugged.

'Perhaps it was some private interest.'

'Perhaps it was,' said Owen.

A pretty good day's work so far, thought Owen: and to keep it like that he went to see Zeinab.

'Well,' he said, 'it's all fixed up. Tomorrow!'

'I don't know that I want to come, really,' said Zeinab.

'Jesus!' exploded Owen. 'Just when I've spent the whole morning arranging –'

'Don't you have any work to do?'

'You are priority,' said Owen cunningly.

'I wish I could believe that.'

'You can, you can! That's the point of the whole thing, to get away somewhere where there are no distractions, just you and me –'

'There is that to be said for the place, I suppose,' said Zeinab. 'There will certainly be no distractions.'

'That's the point! That's just the point!'

'Well –' said Zeinab, softening.

Then she sat back up.

'You mean I might possibly have your undivided attention for two whole days?' she demanded.

'Sure, sure –' he said, kissing her.

'Not just for short, concentrated bursts?' said Zeinab, lying back.

Owen collected the next day's newspapers, all of them now, and settled down in his usual place in the café. Fewer people than usual interrupted him this evening and he was glad of that because he wanted to get back to Zeinab.

Suddenly he saw Mahmoud hurrying towards him. He had a slip of paper in his hand. He laid it before Owen. It was a transcription of a message telegraphed that afternoon from Medinet. It was addressed to Mahmoud and read:

Esteemed El Zaki Effendi: have honour to inform you that this day have apprehended dreadful assassin of Tvardovsky Effendi.

(Signed) Ali Mudina, Mudir.

'I was going to the Fayoum tomorrow anyway,' said Owen, staring at the slip. 'But –'

Mahmoud was already there on the platform. So, as it happened, was Savinkov. As well, strangely, was Prince Fuad, who was pacing up and down moodily, his hands in his pockets. He turned in surprise.

'Hello,' he said, 'you going down too? Fancy a bit of shooting?'

Zeinab threw down her bag in disgust.

'Are there any more of them?' she said. 'Is this your idea of a holiday?'

12

'It won't take long,' pleaded Owen.

'If you think,' said Zeinab, 'that I am going to hang around by myself all morning in a dump like this, then you are mistaken.'

'There are some nice old things to see –'

'In skirts,' said Zeinab. 'And they are not old.'

'Bridges, water-wheels –'

'I'd rather have the pelicans. How do I get to that goddamned hotel?'

'You catch the train to Abchaway and then take a carriage –'

He settled her in the train.

'You're probably right. It'll be much cooler there. Make yourself comfortable –'

'I will,' promised Zeinab. 'With every man in sight.'

'But I know this man!'

'Very likely, Your Excellency. He is a most notorious villain.'

It was the waiter from the hotel by the lake, the man who had chatted away to Owen that morning by the lake when the financiers were talking.

'But –'

'Effendi!' cried the waiter. 'The man is crazy! He seized me and told me he would beat me if I didn't confess. And then when I confessed, he beat me!'

'That was because you confessed to the wrong things, Fazal!'

156

'Mudir,' said Mahmoud wearily, 'on what grounds are you holding this man?'

'Effendi, he has said bad words.'

'No doubt. However –'

'Not just on this but on many other occasions. Many times he has said: "The effendis are bleeding our country white. They must go."'

'These are foolish words. However –'

'And then, after the Effendi died, he said: "One down, only a hundred thousand to go!"'

'Foolish words, too. And wrong. However –'

' "Did I not tell you," he said, "that a blow would be struck? Well, now it has been." '

'When were these words spoken?'

'After the Effendi had died. It was that very day, after all the mighty had departed. Abu heard him, and Sayid heard him, and Ibrahim, and –'

'The cruel words by themselves are nothing: but what was that he also said? That a blow *would be* struck? When did he say that?'

'Before the effendis came. When the hotel was getting ready. All were working hard, and some waxed wrathful. "Why are we doing all this?" they asked. "Just for a bunch of foreign effendis?" And it was then that he said it. "Don't you worry," he said. "They've got it coming to them. A blow will be struck which will shake them in their shoes."'

'Those words are interesting.'

The Mudir's chest swelled.

'That is what I thought, Effendi. I said to myself, those other words are but wind. They are what any foolish man might say. But to speak thus beforehand argues not foolishness but knowledge.'

'Your thoughts are not unwise.' Mahmoud turned to the waiter. 'Fazal, did you speak those words?'

The waiter swallowed.

'Effendi, I did.'

'Then I think you must tell us what made you speak thus.'

'Effendi –'

The waiter stopped.

'Effendi,' he started again. 'Effendi, it so befell that one day I was walking beside the lake –'

'Oh, yes!' said the Mudir sceptically.

'–in the cool of the evening. And I saw a boat approaching across the lake. And it drew into land and two men got out. They asked me in which direction lay the hotel and I said I would lead them to it. On the way we spoke much. And they said: "Do not we know you?" And I said: "I think not." And they said: "Did not we hear you speaking at the cement works?" "That may be so," I said; for, Effendi, I had indeed spoken there some weeks before. I speak, Effendi,' the waiter explained shyly, 'in the Mustapha Kamil cause.'

'Proceed.'

'The men said they had seen me then. "What you said was foolish," they said.'

'They're right, there!' said the Mudir.

'"To speak thus in a house belonging to the Kfouris is foolish," they said. "I spoke not against the Kfouris," I said. "I spoke against the effendis from over the seas."

'"No matter," they said. "You spoke in a house belonging to the Kfouris and they do not like such talk. You had better not go there again." And then, Effendis, I was silent, for they were not men it was wise to argue with. And then, when we had gone a little further and could see the hotel before us, one of them said: "Although to speak thus, in such a place, was foolish, in what you said there was some merit. These foreigners settle on the land like locusts. They eat everything." And I still was silent, Effendi, although in my heart I agreed with them.'

He looked at Mahmoud but Mahmoud's face remained expressionless.

'Go on,' he said.

'Well, Effendi, then the other man spoke. He said: "A plague is coming here: do you know that?" And I said that I knew that we were shortly to make ready for a visitation of foreigners.

And he said: "That is it." And then he asked me if I would like to strike a blow against the locusts. But I said that I was a man of peace. And they both laughed and said: "Stay out of it, then."'

'What did they do when you got to the hotel?'

'They asked me to show them round. And then they went down to look at the boats. And then one of them said: "There will be a shooting of birds, will there not?" And I said that was so. And he said: "It will not just be birds that are shot." And then they went back to their boat.'

'It was the boat that did it,' explained the Mudir. 'When Abu told me what he had said – this was only last Tuesday, at Khabradji's wedding, after we had had a few beers – I went straight across there. "What's this you've been doing?" I said. And he came out with some cock-and-bull story about grapes. And I said: "Right, you bastard, then I'll have to beat it out of you." And it was then that he came out with all this fairy-story stuff. It was when he told me about the boat that I knew he was lying. "A bunch of corsairs?" I said. "What do you think this is? The coast of Barbary?" And so I arrested him.'

Outside the door of the police station the headmaster was waiting with one of his boys.

'Effendis,' he said, 'may I beg the privilege of a teacher and speak on behalf of one of my boys?'

'You certainly may; but should you be speaking to us?'

'I am afraid so, Effendis. It would be useless of me to say he meant no ill, for he plainly did. This only would I say: that there is prospect for good as well as evil in him and that too heavy a hand now may push him irrevocably away from the good. And that there is the prospect of good in him can be seen from the fact that he, of his own accord, came to me and confessed.'

'A teacher's words should be listened to with respect,' said Mahmoud. 'But, O Sheikh, why are they spoken to us?'

'Because you have met the boy and know there is good in him.'

'Met the boy? But –'

They had not recognized him in the school jacket and the turned-up collar. It was the boy for whom the grapes had fallen so opportunely and who had been so helpful to them in providing mounts for their journey to see the excavations and sluices at Hawara.

The boy stepped forward.

'Effendis, I confess!'

'So one should when one has done wrong,' said Mahmoud sternly. 'What is it that you confess to?'

'I might not have confessed if the Mudir had not taken my uncle,' admitted the boy. 'But why should my uncle suffer for wrongs that I have done?'

'You have done!'

The boy squared his shoulders.

'Effendis, it was I who climbed up to the window that night and let the men in.'

'Window?'

Light dawned.

'The old lady's house? You helped the men to break in?'

'Effendis, I did.'

'But why did you do that?' said Mahmoud wrathfully. 'Is she not an old lady and deserving of respect?'

The boy hung his head.

'Effendis, she is, and I have done wrong. But at the time it seemed a bold thing to do and I – I sometimes find it hard not to do bold things. So when the other boys hung back, I said that I would do it. And climbed up to the window.'

'That was very bad.'

'I know it. Afterwards I was troubled in my mind and deliberated whether to go and tell all to the Sheikh. But then when nothing seemed to happen, and the Mudir to be following trails which led in circles and yet wider circles, I thought, perhaps this thing is best forgotten. And I would have said nothing only suddenly he alit on my uncle.'

'You would have done better to have confessed in the first

160

place. However, now that you have, there is the opportunity to turn evil into good.'

'And will my uncle be released?'

'Your uncle is already released.'

The boy bowed his head.

'Effendis, I will do what I can.'

'The men who entered the house that night: tell me about them.'

'There were three: an Effendi and two rough fellows.'

'The Effendi was foreign?'

'He was.'

'And had you seen him before?'

'Effendi, I had. He goes sometimes to the Kfouris. I think he works for them.'

'And the other two?'

'They also.'

'They are evil men,' said Mahmoud. 'Stay out of their way. It need not be for long.'

'I will stay out of Medinet altogether. I will go to my uncle.'

'That would be wise.'

'O, Tarik,' said Owen to the cripple crouched by the railway station gates, 'you who see so much, you who see everyone who comes to Medinet: did you not say to me that there is a foreign effendi who comes to visit the Kfouris, who came in the days just before the Sitt's house was broken into?'

'I did, Effendi.'

'Here is a hard question, for it happened so long ago: did that man also come in the days before the great gathering of the foreign effendis in the hotel by the lake? That gathering in which the foreign effendi died?'

'That is a hard question indeed,' said the cripple. He thought for a moment. 'Effendi, so long afterwards, I cannot be sure. But I think he may have done.'

'Thank you, Tarik.'

161

'Effendi,' said the cripple, as Owen turned to go, 'the man is at the Kfouris now. He came this day, early.'

'Blessing upon you, Tarik. Go in peace.'

'Oh, but you've just missed them!' said Irena Kundasova, when he called at her house. 'They went out only a short time ago.'

'Where have they gone?'

'Well, they were going to see two of Boris's business associates. In fact, they had a bit of a quarrel. Boris wanted to go by himself but Natasha insisted on going with him. "You've only got yourself to blame, Boris," I told him. "You're always going over to see them, when you should be having dinner here. Or at least looking after Natasha." "I can look after myself," said Natasha. And she insisted on going with him. But then, do you know what?'

'No?'

'Just at the moment when they were about to set out, someone told Boris that his friends would be away. They had a business meeting, it appeared, over at Abouxah and wouldn't be back till the evening. Well, Boris was quite put out. "What are we going to do now?" he said to Natasha. "Wait till they get back, I suppose," she said.

'And then I had an idea. "Why don't you take her out to lunch?" I said. "Yes, why don't you?" said Natasha. "We could go to that hotel by the lake, the one you wanted to buy." He had made an offer for it, you know, but then when it came to the point, he found that someone else had just bought it.

'And do you know who that person was? Tvardovsky! Well, when Boris found out he laughed and laughed. "This one too?" he said. "That Tvardovsky! There's no stopping him." But I don't think he minded, really. Anyway, that's where they've gone. "It will make up for your neglect of her," I said. Isn't that lovely?'

Not so lovely, thought Owen, remembering that Zeinab would be there when Natasha arrived.

* * *

162

Owen returned to the police station. It was empty. The Mudir had gone with Mahmoud to pick up the two fellahin the boy had described. They worked at the Kfouri cement works on the edge of the town, the Mudir said. 'It will not take long,' he had assured them.

Long enough, thought Owen, glancing at his watch. He would miss the next train now. Zeinab would be beginning to bridle. Still, if he could get all this sorted out before he left then he would be able to concentrate on her for the rest of the weekend. Where was Mahmoud?

It was very hot in the police station and after a while he wandered out in search of air. His stroll took him in the direction of the railway station, where, at the station gates, the cripple was sitting in the shade of a lebbek tree.

'Effendi,' said the cripple, 'the boy should be looked to.'

Owen crouched down beside him.

'He has gone to stay with his uncle.'

'I know,' said Tarik. 'I saw him leave on the train.'

'I was afraid he might not be able to afford a ticket.'

'He was sitting on an axle.'

Tarik raised his hand hastily.

'It is all right, Effendi. The boys do that often. It is not that I am afraid of. Effendi, you spoke to the boy outside the police station. Where all could hear. There was a man of the Kfouris nearby. I think he may have heard and gone to tell his masters.'

'Thank you, Tarik. I think it should be all right. My friend has gone with the Mudir to lay hold of those two bad men.'

'That is good, Effendi. But the Kfouris have other men. It would be well to look to the boy. And to his uncle.'

'Your warning is wise. Go now to the station master and say that no train is to leave until the Mamur Zapt bids.'

The cripple nodded, and loped off with his strange, hyena-like gait. Owen returned to the police station. He found some keys in a desk and then began to work through the station's cupboards.

At last he found what he wanted: a handgun, old and

163

outdated, but at least it was a service model, one with which he was familiar. He found some bullets in another cupboard and loaded them into the gun. Then he slipped it into his pocket.

Mahmoud came into the room, cross.

'They're not there,' he said. 'We've just missed them. Someone said they'd gone off with a foreign effendi.'

'We need to find them, quick,' said Owen.

'That's not going to be easy,' said Mahmoud. 'They went off in a boat.'

The engine sped along the line. In the cab the heat was terrific. Water was the problem, said the driver. They would have to stop for water. They did. A great arm swung out from a wider tank and the stoker climbed up on top of the engine to feed the pipe in. Owen and Mahmoud chafed.

In truth, it did not take long. The stoker pushed the arm back and clambered down and in a moment the engine was speeding along again.

Surprised signalmen, solitary Arabs on their camels, the odd boy working a water-wheel on his buffalo, all whizzed past. At last they saw the halt of Abchaway ahead of them.

They jumped down and ran to the row of waiting cabs.

'Who is the fastest among you?'

They all opened their mouths.

'Point,' said Mahmoud. 'Do not speak.'

They climbed in. The driver whipped his horses and the cab shot away. At any time the road would have been rough; taken at speed, it threw the cab about wildly. As long as it did not break down!

They drove through orchards heavy with fruit, between fields ripe with corn, giant heads through which the faces of small boys peeped thunderstruck, then beside a stretch of canal along the edge of which the cab skeetered crazily. And then ahead of them they saw the blue streak of the lake.

A few of the guests were still sitting at table. Savinkov

and Natasha, latecomers, were halfway through their meal. Zeinab was sitting solitary at another table, her back turned pointedly on proceedings and especially on Natasha. Prince Fuad, lingering over coffee and obviously finding the taste bitter, looked up in surprise. Waiters were scurrying to and fro.

Mahmoud ran across to the maître d'hôtel.

'Where is Fazal?' he said urgently.

At that moment the waiter came out of the kitchen carrying a tray.

'Get into the house!' said Mahmoud. 'Stay there! Lock him in,' he said to the maître d'hôtel, 'and see that no one gets to him. Where is the boy?' he said to Fazal.

'The boy?' The waiter looked bewildered.

'Your nephew. Has he got here yet?'

'Oh, yes. He's – he went for a walk. Down there.' He pointed down to the lake. 'I told him to go and play there until I was free –'

'Where is he?'

The boy was nowhere to be seen.

'What's going on?' said Fuad, getting up from the table.

'The boy – they're after him!'

'Who are?' said Fuad.

'The men who killed Tvardovsky,' said Mahmoud over his shoulder as he ran down towards the reeds.

And then, in Owen's racing perceptions, events seemed suddenly to lurch.

'Killed Tvardovsky?' said Savinkov, springing up and putting his hand inside his jacket. He set off after Mahmoud.

'Shooting, eh,' said Prince Fuad interestedly. He plunged into a nearby tent and emerged with a rifle. 'How many?'

'Two,' said Owen. 'Fellahin. And perhaps one foreigner, if Tobin is with them. But –'

Fuad raced off.

'Tobin?' said Natasha. 'The Okhrana?'

She pulled out a gun and set off.

Owen started after her.

'Where do you think you're going?' said Zeinab, jumping up.

Down on the foreshore things stabilized for a moment. Mahmoud, surrounded by a crowd of agitated boatmen, was scanning the reeds.

'He's out there somewhere. He was watching the boat coming in and when he saw the men he ran into the reeds.'

'Where are the men?'

'They're in there too.'

And then they lurched again.

'The men who killed Tvardovsky?' said Savinkov, his face set and now with a gun in his hand. He stepped into the water and waded in among the head-high reeds. In a second he had disappeared from sight.

Owen took out his revolver.

'How many men?'

'Three.'

'Tobin!' said Natasha, splashing into the lake. The reeds closed behind her.

Owen reached out to stop her. The next moment the gun was snatched from his hand and he found himself sprawling in the water, pushed there by Zeinab.

'If you think you're going into the reeds with her –!' said Zeinab.

She pushed the reeds apart with Owen's gun and slid in among them.

'I'll get that bitch!' she swore.

'Do you know?' said Fuad, looking at the rifle he held in his hands, 'I think they're right. This kind of thing is no good for close-quarters work. Still –'

He shrugged and went off; at first along the shore side of the reeds, then plunging in at a tangent.

Things stabilized once more; roughly.

166

Mahmoud, gunless, entered the reeds too, moving through them systematically and calling out:

'Ibrahim! This is the Parquet. Stay where you are. We are searching for those men. Stay hidden until I shout!'

Owen, also gunless now, picked himself up out of the water. Taller than the rest, he was able to look out over the sea of reeds. Far off, in the middle of the patch, he thought he saw some bulrush heads moving, and set off towards them.

Almost at once he lost his sense of direction. His feet sank into the ooze and pulled him down so that he could no longer see over the tops of the reeds. Little insects rose in swarms from the reeds and the tangles of convolvulus among them. They settled on his face, his arms, his neck. Looking down, he saw his jacket front black with them. The smell of stagnant mud was everywhere, made worse as his feet disturbed the ooze. The reeds closed about him and it was as it had been on that day when he and Tvardovsky had pushed off in their low, half-submerged boats and seen the birds flying above them.

He realized suddenly that this was a pointless exercise. In this morass of reeds, where there were no signposts, no paths, no distinguishing features, just reeds and more reeds, and the water and mud beneath and the sky above, you would never find anyone except by accident. How had they found Tvardovsky that day? They must have waited in the reeds by the shore and then followed his boat in.

Over to his right he could hear someone blundering and wondered for a moment whether to go over to them. Then he thought how he might be received, coming at them out of the reeds, and stopped still. If they heard him moving they might still fire. He wondered whether to call out.

Then, suddenly, over to his left, he heard a shot. It echoed and re-echoed across the lake and birds rose in their hundreds.

He knew at once whose gun it was and set out stumbling towards it. It was the big service revolver, the one Zeinab had taken from him.

167

'Zeinab!' he cried. 'Zeinab!'

He pushed through the reeds and there she was sitting in the water.

'Zeinab!'

'I've broken my arm!' she said stupidly, looking at her right forearm.

He knelt down in the mud beside her.

'It was when I fired! It just – broke my arm.'

'You stupid idiot!' he cursed. He fished in the water and found the gun. 'You don't know how to use these things!'

'I'll use a knife next time!' Zeinab promised grimly.

She got to her feet.

It was the recoil, and probably just a sprain.

'What were you firing at?'

'A man.'

She pointed.

'Right, now get the hell out of here and leave it to me!'

'Which way?' said Zeinab contritely, nursing her arm.

Owen tried to work it out and couldn't.

'You'd better stay here,' he said. 'Stay here until I shout!'

He took the gun and waded off in the direction she had pointed in. The gun, after its immersion, would be useless, but he had a vague feeling that he might threaten with it, or club with it.

Ahead of him he heard a shot, and then a cry.

And then another cry.

'Where is he?' shouted Natasha.

He blundered towards her.

The gun fired again and this time he heard the whistle of the bullet.

'It's me, you damned fool! Stop firing!'

He came out of the reeds into a little shallow pool, in the middle of which Natasha was standing.

'Where is he?' she cried.

'Who?'

'Tobin. I saw him.'

'Did you hit him?'

168

'He cried out, and then I lost him.'

'Did you hit him?'

'I think so.'

She had hit him. There, when he pushed cautiously through the reeds, were fresh drops of blood.

'Keep out of it!' he said, pushing her behind him. A moment later, however, he found her following him.

They moved carefully forward. Natasha suddenly pointed. There was another drop of blood.

They followed the trail slowly. It became easier to follow. The reeds were bent down as if he had rushed away in a panic. Some of the reeds were spiked with blood and in one place there was a little puddle of it.

Then, suddenly, ahead of them was a voice.

'Don't!' it pleaded. 'Don't!'

'Where are they?' said another voice. It was Savinkov's.

Owen and Natasha came out from the reeds. Tobin was half sitting, half kneeling in the water. He was holding a great red patch that ran all the way down his side.

Natasha pointed her gun.

'No!' said Owen, and knocked it out of her hand.

It fell into the water, and Natasha scrabbled for it.

'Leave him!' said Owen.

'It's not him I want,' said Savinkov.

'Leave the others to me. You stay here. See she doesn't do anything to him.'

Savinkov hesitated, then lowered his gun.

'Which way?' said Owen.

Tobin pointed dumbly.

Natasha brought the gun up out of the water, aimed it at Tobin and pressed the trigger.

Nothing happened.

Natasha swore and pressed it again. Savinkov came across and took the gun from her.

'Enough!' he said.

Owen set off through the reeds. There was nothing to guide him this time and as soon as he had gone a few steps

169

he stopped, then proceeded more slowly, letting his ears, not his eyes, be his guide.

The birds were still making alarmed cries overhead but he was able to shut out those and listen only to the noises of the reeds, the rustles made by the wind, the gentle plopping of the water, even, eventually, the humming of the insects. What he was listening for was the sucking of footsteps, of feet drawing themselves out of the mud, of the faint splash and plop as they were put down again.

He moved a little way forward, stopped and listened; then moved forward again and listened again.

Everything had become suddenly very quiet. There were no cries, no further shots. Even Mahmoud's voice had died away. They had all heard the shots; he guessed that they would all be doing what he was doing: waiting.

Although it was very quiet, the reeds themselves were not quiet. The rustling of the wind, the lapping of the water, continued. The whines and hums of the insects seemed to be rising to a crescendo.

And then he heard, very soft, the sounds he had been waiting for.

He moved towards them.

His own feet, he knew, would be making the same sounds. He tried to lift them and put them down as noiselessly as he could but every so often there would be an extra loud splash or plop, after which, each time, he held his breath, balancing precariously, sometimes on one leg, until he felt that the silence had resumed.

In the reeds the heat was intense. Sweat was running down his face. He could feel his jacket sticking to his back. At times, when there was a little open patch of water, the sunlight, flashing in it, was almost blinding.

He stopped, after one such moment, to rub the sweat out of his eyes, and was just about to move forward again when he heard, as distinct as a fish plopping, the suck of mud.

He froze where he was and crouched down.

The reeds in front of him parted suddenly and a face

appeared, a turbaned dark face with scars running down the cheeks.

The man's eyes widened and Owen saw the gun come up.

He hurled himself forward.

But, as the reeds broke apart, he saw that there was not one man but two, and both held guns, and he could never reach them, and the shots cracked out –

And then, miraculously, he was lying in the mud looking up at them, and one man was already crumpling and the other man was standing there very still; he seemed to stand there for an eternity, and then the gun slipped from his hands and fell into the water, and then he fell on to his knees and bent forward and continued falling until he, too, slid into the water.

13

'Got the brace, I think,' said Prince Fuad with satisfaction.

He reached down, gave Owen a hand and hauled him up.

'But wasn't there another?' he said enthusiastically.

'The Russian woman's got him.'

Less definitely than Prince Fuad. Owen found Tobin sitting in the water with his back against a clump of reeds, his face very pale, his hand clasped to his side. Beside him crouched Savinkov, talking earnestly to Natasha. He looked up at Owen.

'I have been telling her,' he said, 'that she must forget about the others. They will get their desserts.'

'They already have,' said Owen.

Natasha seemed to relax, although she looked at Tobin in a way that made him flinch.

'Him, too,' said Savinkov.

'I didn't kill Tvardovsky,' whispered Tobin. 'I wasn't even with them that time.'

'You set it up,' said Owen. 'You told them about the shooting party. You may even have arranged for the shooting party in the first place.'

'It would have happened anyway,' whimpered Tobin. 'They had made up their minds.'

From across the reeds came a shout.

'Have you got him?'

It was Mahmoud.

'He's here with Savinkov!'

Mahmoud came splashing through the reeds. He looked down at Tobin. Then he turned away, cupped his hands round his lips, and shouted:

'Ya Ibrahim! It is I, Mahmoud, who speak. We have the men. You can come out now!'

He waited.

'Ya Ibrahim! It is all over. The Parquet is here, and the Mamur Zapt. You can come out now. Shout, if you hear me!'

After a moment, surprisingly near, there came a rather quavery cry.

'Good! Come this way. You are safe. The men cannot harm you.'

They heard the reeds move and the mud sucking and then there was the sound of footsteps stumbling towards them. A moment later, the boy appeared.

Mahmoud embraced him.

'All is well, little brother,' he said.

The boy hid his head against Mahmoud's jacket.

'I lay in the mud,' he said. 'They would have found me only if they'd walked on me.'

'It is well,' said Mahmoud. 'It is well.'

He glanced down at Tobin.

'Let's get them out. I left Fuad with the bodies.' He raised his voice. 'O, Prince! I am going out now. I will send men. Wait but a while!'

Fuad shouted in acknowledgement. Then, with Owen and Mahmoud supporting Tobin, they made their way back through the reeds.

They laid Tobin down in the shade of a boat and Mahmoud sent boatmen to fetch the bodies. Owen went back into the reeds to find Zeinab. Able to shout now, he found her without difficulty.

'So,' she said, looking at him with her fierce possessiveness, 'you are all right; and they are not.'

Owen nodded.

'I took your gun,' she said. 'I shouldn't have done that.

I should have waited until she came out and then used a knife.'

'You don't need to use either. She loved Tvardovsky. And now she is Savinkov's.'

'Not yours?'

'As far as I am concerned,' said Owen, 'she is almost eighty!'

There was no doctor at the hotel and they sent to Medinet for one. They thought it was better to do that than to move him, although Prince Fuad, examining the wound, pronounced it a mere scratch. It was more than that. The bullet had ploughed a furrow round Tobin's left side, narrowly missing the heart.

Fuad was impressed.

'Another two inches and she'd have done it,' he confided to Owen. 'Good shooting – if she meant it!'

'Oh, I think she meant it,' said Owen.

Tobin thought so, too, and eyed Natasha anxiously as he lay beside the boat.

Mahmoud was standing looking out across the lake. The sunlight was so bright on the water it was almost blinding. Owen went down and stood beside him. He knew what he was thinking.

'He'll go for a Consular Court,' he said.

'Yes.'

Under the Capitulations, any foreign national accused of a crime had a right to be tried in a court arranged by his own Consul. Often the case was heard not in Egypt but in the national's own country. Thus an Italian accused of a crime would go to Ancona, in Italy, to be tried, along with all witnesses; a Greek, to Athens, and so on. And, of course, the cases would be heard not under Egyptian law but under the law of that country. The scope for evasion and delay was immense.

'We won't even be able to get him to give evidence against the Kfouris,' said Owen.

'No.'

'A written statement, perhaps?'

'If he'll give it.'

'If he'll give it!' said Owen bitterly.

Mahmoud looked at him.

'Now you know what the Capitulations feel like to an Egyptian,' he said.

Owen went back up the shore and sat down beside Tobin.

'When is the doctor coming?' whispered Tobin.

'Soon.'

'I need to speak to my Consul,' said the Russian fretfully.

'You'll be able to. Actually,' said Owen, 'I need to speak to him too. There are some things I want to ask him.'

'He knows nothing.'

'That, as a matter of fact, was what I wanted to ask him. How much did he know about all this? Take that time when you searched Tvardovsky's rooms: you had policemen with you. That must have been at his request. But did he know what you were searching for?'

He waited. Tobin merely turned his head away.

'Did he know that you were searching for share certificates?'

'Share certificates?' said Fuad.

'Yes, Prince, yours among them. And other things, too. Title deeds to land, that sort of thing. The Kfouris wanted to get hold of them, you see. It was part of their battle with Tvardovsky. But I don't think the Consul knew that. I think he thought it was something to do with Strakhov. Okhrana business.'

'Okhrana?' said Natasha, stirring.

Owen turned to her.

'Yes,' he said. 'Tobin worked for both. I don't think the Consul knew that, either. He knew that Tobin worked for the Okhrana but he didn't know he also worked, privately, for the Kfouris. I don't think he'll be too pleased about that.'

'I'll take my chance,' said Tobin.

'And what about your raid on Irena Kundasova's house in the Fayoum? Was that done in your capacity as Okhrana agent? Or were you working for the Kfouris then?'

'He raided Irena?' said Natasha.

'We needed the certificates,' said Tobin. 'We thought that Tvardovsky might have left them with her.'

'That was your role, wasn't it?' said Owen. 'Tracking down the certificates and getting hold of them. Not work the others could do. Unlike Tvardovsky's killing. But even there you supplied the information.'

'Okhrana swine!' said Natasha.

Tobin looked away.

'In fact, I suspect there'll be quite a lot of things your Consul doesn't know. And when he finds out about them, I don't think he's going to be very happy. Or your government, either.'

'Why are you saying this?'

'They might leave you on your own.'

Tobin was silent for quite some time. Then he said:

'So?'

'I thought we might do a deal.'

'What kind of deal?'

'You're not going to let this bastard go!' said Natasha incredulously.

'From you, a signed statement about your dealings with the Kfouris.'

'And from you?'

'A guarantee that we will not make any difficulties about any application for your case to be heard in the Consular Courts.'

Tobin laughed.

'That all?' He heaved himself round so that he was facing Owen. 'You don't have any choice,' he said. 'I know my rights; and I know you can't touch me.'

'Can't touch him?' said Prince Fuad indignantly. 'What is all this?'

176

'I'm afraid it's true, Prince. He's got the law on his side.'

'Law?' said Prince Fuad. 'Who makes the law around here? I do.'

'That certainly used to be true, Prince, but these days there are all sorts of restrictions. The Capitulations –'

'Capitulations?' said the Prince. 'Thought they were to do with money?'

'Well, they are, Prince. But –'

'You go to the bank and ask for a loan, and they put conditions on it. Ask for a palace or two as security. Nothing wrong with that. That's the way it always has been and always will be. But what's that got to do with this chap?'

'Well, one thing leads to another, Prince, and the way things have ended up, foreigners have acquired certain privileges –'

'You mean, you can't touch them?'

'I'm afraid that's right, Prince.'

'Dammit,' said the Prince, 'whose country is it? Mine or theirs?'

'Well, Prince, I'm afraid that these days –'

The doctor arrived at last and with him the Mudir. Owen took the Mudir across to show him the bodies.

'Two!' said the Mudir.

'That's right,' said Prince Fuad. 'Got them both.'

The Mudir looked at him hesitantly.

'Accident?' he suggested tentatively.

'No accident about it!' said the Prince indignantly. 'Just damned good shooting!'

'Yes, Your Excellency,' said the Mudir humbly. 'Of course, Your Excellency!'

He looked a little worried, however.

'Excellency –'

'Yes?'

'What shall I put in my report?'

'Put what you damned well like!'

Owen intervened.

177

'There's no need for you to say anything. I'll handle this.'

'Thank you, Effendi!' said the Mudir, grateful and relieved. Then, spirits reviving rapidly. 'Of course, Effendi! What need is there to say anything? Such trash as this! Pooh! What is a mere fellah here or there? To one such as His Excellency? Quite right, Effendi! Best to forget all about it.'

His eye fell on Tobin.

'Another!'

He reeled.

'And an effendi, too!'

He looked more closely.

'A foreign effendi! Excellency –'

'Well?' said Prince Fuad.

The Mudir swallowed.

'Accident?' he said feebly. 'Another one?'

'Accident?' said Prince Fuad thoughtfully, looking at Tobin. 'No. Not yet.'

'Here,' said Tobin, looking first at Fuad and then at Natasha, whose eyes had never left him, 'you're not going to leave me with those two!'

'No,' said Owen regretfully. 'But someone will have to take charge of you while we go after the Kfouris.'

'What was that you said about a statement?' said Tobin.

The statement was useful later in securing a conviction for the Kfouris. To their indignation – even when supplemented by a host of details which, in their fury, they were only too ready to supply – it did not secure as much for Tobin. This was because he elected to go, as Owen and Mahmoud had supposed, for trial in a Consular Court. The case was heard in Odessa; or would have been heard had it not been transferred to Sebastopol; whereupon it was transferred – And the last Owen heard was that it was being transferred still.

There was, however, some relief for Mahmoud over the Capitulations. The appeal in the De Vries and Boutigny case was not sustained; and this success turned out to herald the end of the entire system.

'A quiet weekend in the Fayoum?' said the Financial Adviser, sipping his whisky, a few days after their return to Cairo.

'Actually, it wasn't so quiet,' Owen objected mildly.

After Tobin had handed him his statement, he and Mahmoud had gone immediately to call on the Kfouris. They had found them just on the brink of departing. Depart, later, they did, but in handcuffs and accompanied by Mahmoud and the Mudir, and bound for a jail in Cairo; but what this meant was that by the time Owen got back to the hotel, it was well into the evening and he was saved from Zeinab's wrath only by Savinkov hurriedly inviting them to join him in a late but splendid supper.

Even this had not been plain sailing, for the company had naturally included Natasha. Fortunately, it had also included Prince Fuad. The Prince was much taken by Natasha ('You've got to allow for the reeds, Owen: another two inches and she'd have got him bang through the middle. I call that very respectable.') and the compliments he paid her, each of which, Zeinab fondly imagined, was like a dagger through Owen's heart, had brightened her mood considerably.

Her cheerfulness was further increased the next day when they went to lunch at Irena Kundasova's and she found that there really was an eighty-year-old lady. Moreover, reminded by Natasha's affection for her of the mother that she herself had somehow mislaid on her passage through life, she was unaccountably touched; and she and Natasha ended up by exchanging tearful embraces on the platform at Medinet.

Medinet itself, however, had fallen short of her expectations. Venice it was not. Here, though, the prospect of improvement happily unveiled itself, for Savinkov, who had a place in the real Venice, invited them to join him there.

At once, though, to Zeinab's fury, the prospect was dashed by Owen remarking, somewhat huffily in Zeinab's opinion, that a British government official could not accept favours.

If that was so, Zeinab inquired, what was the point of being an official?

She had gone on, in the train on their way back to Cairo, to link this to the general state of his finances. When, she had asked, would he be in a position to support her in the style of life to which she would like to be accustomed? And if, as seemed more than likely given government levels of pay, the answer was, 'Never', what was he going to do about it?

Owen, considering how he might reply, found himself plunging for a moment into a world of Tvardovskean financial chimera, a world in which, while the distant horizon was bright and clear, the ground between was dark and obscure.

It was at times like this that one needed advice. Prince Fuad had been right; what he needed was a sympathetic banker. But the sympathetic banker, alas, was dead, as they always are, and he knew that if he went to the ordinary sort, to Jarvis, say, he would be fobbed off with some remark about a formula; and he, sadly, had no palaces to offer.

The thought came to him that there was a difference between low finance and high finance. In the world of low finance you couldn't get away with anything. In the world of high finance you could – sometimes – get away with murder.